THE SECRETS OF GRIM WOOD

LOWTHAR'S BLADE TRILOGY
❋ BOOK 2 ❋

THE SECRETS OF GRIM WOOD

R. L. LaFevers

DUTTON CHILDREN'S BOOKS · NEW YORK

Copyright © 2005 by R. L. LaFevers

Library of Congress Cataloging-in-Publication Data
LaFevers, R. L. (Robin L.)
The secrets of Grim Wood/by R.L. LaFevers.—1st ed.
p. cm.
Summary: Young Kenric is entrusted with three magic stones to help him in forging an alliance between the humans, the Fey, and the goblins, a task which turns out to be as difficult and dangerous as he fears.
ISBN 0-525-47372-6
[1. Magic—Fiction. 2. Fantasy.] I. Title.
PZ7.L1414Se   2005
[Fic]—dc22   2004017447

Published in the United States by Dutton Children's Books,
a division of Penguin Young Readers Group
345 Hudson Street, New York, New York 10014
www.penguin.com/youngreaders

Printed in USA
Map and title-page art by Hunter Brown
First Edition
1 3 5 7 9 10 8 6 4 2

To my mother, Dixie Young,
who has treated every word I have ever written as sacred
lore and whose library is bigger than Rindelorn's.
She always has exactly the right book when I need it.

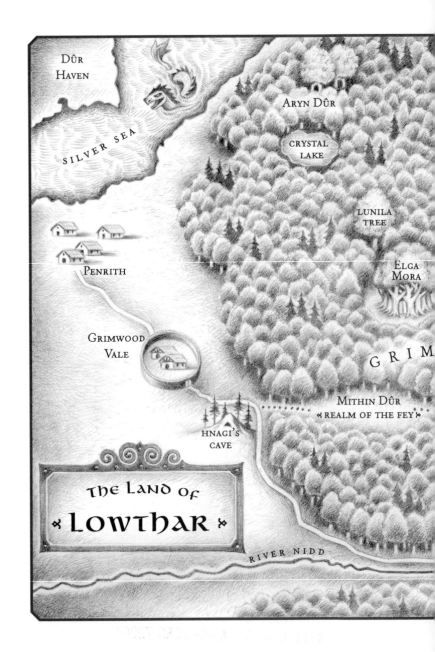

DÛR
HAVEN

SILVER SEA

ARYN DÛR

CRYSTAL
LAKE

LUNILA
TREE

ELGA
MORA

PENRITH

GRIMWOOD
VALE

G R I M

MITHIN DÛR
❧ REALM OF THE FEY ❧

HNAGI'S
CAVE

THE LAND OF
❧ LOWTHAR ❧

RIVER NIDD

LOWTHAR'S BLADE TRILOGY · BOOK 2

THE SECRETS OF GRIM WOOD

❄ I ❄

Kenric struggled against the iron grip that held him. He watched in horror as the sharp point of the sword drew closer to his hand. Mordig's face loomed, evil and mocking. Kenric's father called out his name, begging Mordig for mercy. But Mordig had no mercy in him. A sharp, burning pain slashed across Kenric's palm.

Kenric jerked awake. His heart was pounding, and he was drenched in sweat. His hand throbbed where he'd been cut three days ago. Mordig had kidnapped Kenric's father and forced him to forge a powerful sword. When Kenric had tried to interfere, Mordig had demanded his blood in order to try and awaken the power in the blade.

It has worked, and Kenric had managed to use the

power of the blade to save his father and imprison Mordig. But it had been close. Too close. None of them had escaped unharmed.

As Kenric's racing heart slowed, he saw the first light of dawn peeking through the window. It was time to be on his way.

He wasn't sure how he felt about this newest task for the king. Setting out to find his father had been one thing. He would have done anything to get him back. But now that his father was safe, all Kenric wanted to do was return home and enjoy being a family again. But that was not to be. Instead, he was on his way back to Grim Wood, the home of the Fey.

He sighed, rolled out of bed, and began to dress. The Fey didn't care for outsiders. They had made it very clear that Kenric wasn't welcome in Grim Wood. But the king had insisted. He had a task he wanted Kenric to do for him. Several tasks, actually.

When Kenric had finished dressing, he grabbed his pack and put it on. He opened his chamber door and stepped out into the hallway, where he tripped over something and stumbled. He looked down and saw a bundle lying on the floor. The bundle sat up. It was small, smaller than Kenric, and had large pointed ears. It was the color of swamp mud and had very pointed teeth.

"Hnagi? What are you doing here?" Kenric had a soft spot for the little goblin. Hnagi had tried so hard to help Kenric on his journey. Of course, he'd ended up being more trouble than help. But his heart had been in the right place.

The little goblin sprang to his feet. "Waiting for Kenric. Want firestone back."

Kenric winced. "The king says I have to keep it for a while longer, Hnagi. He thinks I might need the stones' power on this next journey."

"Firestone Hnagi's."

"I know it's yours," Kenric said. "As soon as I've finished this task for the king, I'll give it right back. I promise."

Hnagi scowled. "Hnagi see firestone. Want to see it safe."

"All right." Kenric pulled the small leather pouch out of his pocket.

Hnagi was suddenly next to him, his nose pressed up against the pouch.

"The moonstone's in there, too, so watch it." Hnagi jerked his hand back so the moonstone wouldn't burn him.

Kenric took the firestone out. He held it between two fingers and watched the pale gold strands flicker in its depths.

Hnagi reached out with one finger and stroked the small stone. When the goblin touched it, the gold flared to fiery orange streaks that blazed deep inside the blue stone.

Hnagi threw Kenric a sly look, and his fingers twitched. Immediately, Kenric snatched the stone back and shoved it into the pouch. "Don't even think it," he said.

Hnagi folded his arms. "Firestone Hnagi's," he repeated stubbornly.

Kenric sighed. "I know. And I'm really sorry. But I can't give it back yet."

Still glaring, the goblin said, "Where firestone go, Hnagi go. Not let stone out of sight."

Kenric rubbed his face. Hnagi was making this so much harder. "You don't understand. I have to go back to the Fey and talk to them for the king. You don't want to come with me." The goblin hated the wild, mysterious race who lived in Grim Wood—and they hated him.

"Hnagi go where stone go," he insisted.

"Very well," Kenric said with a sigh. Hnagi had a rare talent for making a bad situation worse.

THE CASTLE DOORS had been thrown open for the last three days to let in light and air. Kenric also suspected it was to allow any dark things to skulk away. He couldn't help but marvel at how much had changed in those days. Ever since Kenric had used the power of the stones to trap Mordig, the whole castle seemed lighter. Even the town seemed brighter. It was as if a heavy cloud of fear had been lifted. Shadows no longer seemed to lurk in every corner. Men no longer looked at one another with suspicion. Kenric felt proud that he'd had something to do with this.

He spotted the king talking to his father as they waited for him.

Kenric's father seemed to be back to his old self now that he'd been freed from Mordig's prison. The long shadows and sorrow were gone from his face. His eyes no longer looked dull and hopeless.

As the king greeted him, Kenric was struck by how old and tired he looked. Putting a kingdom back together must be hard work, Kenric realized.

"I have come to bid you farewell on your journey, young smith."

"Thank you, Your Majesty."

The king turned back to Kenric's father. "Thank you, Brogan, for giving your son into my service."

Kenric's father nodded at the king's words, but his mouth grew hard. Kenric knew he wasn't happy about Kenric's newest task for the king. But he had no choice. Neither of them did.

The king turned back to Kenric. "Much is riding on your shoulders. It won't be easy to convince the Fey to renew our old alliance. Nor do I think they'll be pleased at your request to search their lore. But there is no help for it. We must learn how to forge a blade of power."

The king paused, and equal parts hope and sorrow shone in his eyes. "And then there is the Princess Tamaril. I can only hope my daughter made it to Grim Wood and is hiding in safety there. I am encouraged by the blood-stone you found. I am certain it is her royal stone."

Kenric's hand went to the pouch that held the princess's bloodstone, along with the other two stones he carried. "Yes, Your Majesty. Hopefully the Fey girl who gave it to me can show me where she found it. That will be a place to start."

"I see your goblin friend goes with you. Anxious about his firestone, no doubt," the king said with a smile.

"Where firestone go, Hnagi goes," the little goblin muttered.

"And you still have the moonstone I gave you?" the king asked Kenric.

"Yes, Your Majesty. It's here with the others."

"Excellent. You will most likely need them on your journey. The kingdom is safer than it was, thanks to you. But my scouts tell me there are still pockets of evil about, so you must be wary."

Kenric's mind immediately flew to the terrifying creatures he knew lurked in the shadows: grymclaws, Mawr hounds, and the Sleäg. He desperately hoped he wouldn't run into any of Mordig's servants on his journey.

"Very well. Then I will bid you farewe—"

A low rumble erupted from somewhere deep within the castle, cutting off the king's words. The earth shifted beneath their feet. The king seemed to flicker, growing faint and wraithlike, then quickly becoming solid again.

As the rumbling stopped, Kenric stepped forward. "Your Majesty! Are you all right?"

The king shook his head to clear it. "Yes, yes. I am fine. But Mordig grows restless in his stone prison." He looked up and met Kenric's eyes. There was no hiding his urgency. "You must hurry!"

⊀ 2 ⊁

KENRIC PLANNED to enjoy this short time with his father. For two long months he'd feared he'd never see him again. Kenric had had to travel into Mordig's stronghold to find him. He'd earned this time with his father, time just to enjoy being together again. Even if it was only for a short while.

The day's journey went by quickly and pleasantly. Kenric filled his father in on all that had happened while he was missing. He explained how Gormley, the landlord, had tried to take their cottage from them. Kenric's father didn't say much, but he kept his arm around Kenric's shoulders, as if afraid to let him go.

Hnagi followed behind like a small thundercloud. As the sun set, they picked a sheltered spot off the side of the road for their campsite. Trying to cheer Hnagi up, Kenric put the goblin in charge of lighting the fire.

After gathering a small pile of kindling, Hnagi opened the pouch at his belt. With a quick flick of his wrist, he tossed his fire-dust onto the wood. There was a *whoosh* as the flames caught and leaped to life. Brogan jerked back in surprise, and Hnagi smiled for the first time that day.

They ate a quick dinner, then lay down on their bedrolls. Kenric waited for sleep to come while Hnagi squatted by the fire, playing with the burning sticks.

There was a faint crackle in the underbrush. Fear tickled the back of Kenric's throat. He rolled to his feet. "Did you hear that?"

"Hear what?" his father asked.

There was more scuffling off behind the trees. Quick as a spark, Hnagi jumped away from the fire and scuttled over to Kenric's side. "That," Kenric said. His mind flew to the large black Mawr hounds that had chased him only days before. Or perhaps it was one of the grymclaws, the evil, winged creatures that hunted the skies. Kenric shuddered at the memory of their talons.

A tall, black-cloaked figure stumbled into view. Fear prickled along Kenric's skin.

"A Sleäg!" his father whispered.

Kenric struggled to shake off the fear that closed in on him. Fear was one of the Sleäg's most powerful weapons. They sucked all the spirit and fight out of whatever they hunted.

Kenric's hand fumbled for the hilt of his knife, which suddenly seemed small and useless against such an enemy. Instead he reached down and grabbed a burning branch from the fire. He forced himself to take a step forward, then another.

"Come back, son! What are you doing?" His father jumped up and tried to grab him.

But before Kenric could step back, the Sleäg reached out a hand toward him. He opened his mouth to speak, but nothing came out. The Sleäg took a step forward, then slowly collapsed onto the forest floor.

Four arrows stuck out of his back. A knife was embedded in his shoulder.

"He's hurt," Kenric said. "I didn't think they *could* be hurt."

"It must be the villagers," Brogan said as he inched closer. "I overheard the guards at the castle. Now that the people have hope again, they are striking out at the Sleäg."

"About time," muttered Kenric. He waited a moment to see if the Sleäg would rise again, but it didn't. He approached the body cautiously, keeping the burning torch in front of him.

As Kenric drew closer, the Sleäg spasmed, then lay still. Kenric stopped and thrust the torch forward. The orange-red light of the flames fell on the Sleäg's face. The flesh was drawn tightly over the skull, making him look more like a skeleton than a man. The eyes were wide open and flickered black and red in the firelight.

The creature struggled once more, then stopped. A foul vapor began to rise off his body. Kenric didn't want it to touch him. He ducked his head under his arm and thrust the torch into the vapor. There was a snap and sizzle. The flame hissed and spat until the last of the mist had vanished.

"What was that?" Kenric asked, backing away.

"I'm not sure. Perhaps Mordig's will has left the creature?" Brogan suggested.

Kenric turned to his father. "How does Mordig get them to do his will in the first place? Surely they know it is wrong."

Brogan sighed and nudged the Sleäg with the toe of

his boot. It didn't move. "They were knights, once. They served the land and their king. But Mordig was able to twist them with his cunning lies. Once the knights were corrupted by power and hate, Mordig took their bound stones from them."

"Their bound stones?" Kenric asked.

Brogan looked down at the still form. "I think he's dead, don't you?"

"I think so," Kenric said.

"Let's move back to the fire and watch for a while to make sure. I'll tell you of the stone binding while we wait."

Kenric and his father made themselves comfortable by the fire. Hnagi crept closer to Kenric and curled up at his side. Brogan began to speak.

"When men of noble blood swear their service to their king, they are also bound to a bloodstone. This symbolizes their loyalty to the land and their king. It is a way of sealing their oath and binding their sense of duty. Mordig figured out that by taking their bound stones, they would be forced to obey him and not the king, so they stopped performing the ceremony. Having a bound stone that Mordig could use against them put the knights at too great a risk."

"But how does holding their stone give Mordig power over them?"

"Once Mordig has taken their stones, he holds the power they have sworn."

As his father's words sank in, an uneasy feeling washed over Kenric. "Is this true whenever a person holds someone else's stone?"

"I believe so, unless it is freely given. But I'm not an expert."

Kenric looked down at Hnagi, lying next to him. His hand crept to the pouch that held the stones. If that were true, it meant that Hnagi was now tied to Kenric's will.

"Is that why you came with us?" he asked the goblin. "Are you bound to your firestone?" Kenric opened the pouch and took the firestone out.

Hnagi shook his head and curled up tighter. "Only royal góblins bound to stones."

"Are you sure? Because if it's true, I don't want that kind of power over you. You can have it back."

Kenric heard his father gasp. Hnagi blinked and sat up. "Ken-ric mean this?"

"Yes, I do." He held the stone out to the little goblin.

Hnagi reached for it, his fingers twitching. He paused. He glanced over at the Sleäg, then back at the stone. His hand dropped back to his side and his ears drooped. "No. King right. Ken-ric need. Much nasty stuff. Hnagi give stone to Ken-ric. But only for short while," he added.

Kenric stared at the goblin. "Are you sure?"

Hnagi gave a firm nod. "Hnagi sure. Want nasty things gone. Then take firestone back."

Kenric put the stone back in his pouch. He was touched by the little goblin's trust.

Brogan glanced over at the Sleäg. "Let's move this body. I'm not sure how much sleep I'll get with it nearby."

Together, Kenric and his father dragged the body far away from the campsite. "Tomorrow before we leave, we'll bury him," Brogan said.

Kenric turned a questioning look to his father. "Why?"

"Because whatever it is now, it was once a man. Whatever evil has befallen him, he deserves that much."

❈ 3 ❈

They got a late start in the morning, slowed down by the time it took to bury the Sleäg. Once they were on the road, they traveled swiftly, trying to make up for lost time. The happy chatter of yesterday was gone. The Sleäg had cast a pall over their small party. Even though Kenric had helped restore the rightful king, they weren't safe yet. They would do well to remember that.

The light was failing when Grim Wood finally came into view. The tangled mass of dark green trees spread out across the land as far as the eye could see. The forest sat watching and waiting, thick with shadows and secrets. Hnagi whimpered.

Kenric turned to him. "Are you sure you don't want to turn back? Go home?"

The goblin shook his head. "Hnagi's home on other side."

"Isn't there someplace safe you could go? Another goblin you could stay with?"

Hnagi shook his head again. "No! Hnagi not go back to góblin realm."

Kenric stared at Hnagi in surprise. "There's a goblin realm?"

Hnagi nodded. "Up north. In mountains of Carreg Dhu. But Hnagi not go back. Besides, Ken-ric might need Hnagi's help. Like last time."

Kenric snorted in disbelief. On their last trip to Grim Wood, the goblin had almost gotten them both killed! Before he could say anything, his father spoke.

"It's late. Do we want to camp here, then enter the forest in the morning?"

Kenric sighed, dreading the moment when they would part ways. He hated letting his father out of his sight. He was afraid he might somehow disappear again. Kenric knew this was foolish, but he couldn't help it. "No. It'll be best if we keep going. The sooner the Fey find us, the better. I want to be done with my business and go home."

Brogan nodded. Kenric adjusted his pack, took a deep breath, then stepped into the woods.

The forest was unnaturally still. It was as if the trees themselves knew unwelcome visitors had entered. Small tendrils of fear crept along Kenric's skin. He wasn't just passing through this time. He needed to find the Fey and talk to them. They had hated letting him pass the last time he was here. If not for the moonstone . . . Kenric stopped walking so suddenly that his father bumped into him.

"What is it, son?"

"I just realized something. We need to guarantee your safe passage through Grim Wood. It won't matter for me. I need to go with the Fey anyway. But you're on your way home to Mother. We don't want the Fey to slow you down or take you prisoner."

"Would they do such a thing? Knowing we came from the king?"

Kenric remembered back to his first meeting with the Fey. The proud, wild creatures had no use for humankind. "I don't think being sent by the king will make any difference," he answered. He reached into his pocket for his small, leather pouch.

Kenric drew the milky white moonstone out and handed it to his father. "This will guarantee your safe passage. The Fey won't hurt you if you carry it."

Brogan pushed Kenric's hand back. "No. The king said you might still need the stones. He meant *all* the stones. You'll need all three for their power to be at its strongest."

True. King Thorgil had wanted him to keep all three stones. But his father had to get home to Mother and the cottage. Gormley was just looking for an excuse to throw her out. The sooner Father got back and put a stop to Gormley's plotting, the better.

"Take it," Kenric said, thrusting the moonstone at his father. "I can't carry out my task if I'm worried about Mother's safety."

Frowning, Brogan reluctantly reached out and took the pale stone from Kenric. He stared at it a moment, then shoved it deep into his pocket.

"Ai! Ai!" Hnagi protested. "You just give nasty Fey stone to father. After Hnagi give you firestone! Stones no good without all three!"

Warmth flooded Kenric's cheeks. What Hnagi said was true. But Kenric was willing to risk the moonstone to make sure his mother was safe. "I'm hoping I'll be able to get another moonstone from the Fey, somehow."

Hnagi clacked his teeth at Kenric and turned away.

A hard knot of guilt lodged itself in Kenric's stomach. "Well, we've wasted enough time. Let's move on." Kenric adjusted his pack, then led the way deeper into the forest.

Twenty paces later, there was a rustling in the branches overhead. Three Fey dropped down from the trees. The dead leaves and bracken on the forest floor erupted. Several more Fey stood up.

Kenric heard his father gasp in shock. Hnagi dove behind Kenric. Nearly a dozen fierce Fey stood in a circle around them, weapons drawn. Kenric immediately recognized the young Fey girl standing in front. Her eyes were the color of new spring grass and her russet brown hair was decorated with twigs and leaves. Her small, thin face was foxlike, and her pale silver dagger pointed directly at his throat.

❧ 4 ❧

"You!" the Fey girl said, eyes narrowed.

"Hello, Linwe," Kenric said.

"Perhaps you misunderstood the first time. You are not welcome here. And he, especially, is not welcome." She nodded her head at Hnagi, who stood quivering behind Kenric's legs.

Kenric sighed. Too bad she hadn't grown any nicer since his last visit.

"Linwe, I'd like you to meet my father, Brogan of Penrith. Father, this is the Fey girl I told you about."

A look of surprise crossed Linwe's face. She flicked her eyes over at Brogan, then back to Kenric. "So, you got him safely away from Mordig."

"Yes. And not onl—"

"Good. Now leave our forest."

"Aren't you curious about what happened to Mordig?" Kenric asked.

"No," she said. "Mordig does not concern us. He has no power here. Our Fey wards and protections are too strong for him."

"Then maybe you can show my king how to—"

"No! We share our secrets with no one." Linwe narrowed her eyes at him. An older Fey man stepped forward. Kenric recognized the captain of the patrol, Faroth, whom he had met last time he was here.

"State your business so we can be done with these games."

"I am sent by King Thorgil," Kenric said. "He wishes me to speak with the Fey on his behalf. There is still much work to be done to put our land back together."

"King Thorgil's wishes do not concern us," said Faroth. Behind him, Linwe nodded her agreement. "Show us your moonstones, and we will let you be on your way."

Kenric shuffled his feet, but kept his eyes on Faroth. "My father carries the moonstone. He is on his way to Penrith. I am staying here until I have seen Cerinor and your Fey king."

Faroth growled. Another Fey nocked an arrow to his bow. Linwe stepped forward, the tip of her dagger an inch from Kenric's throat. "You are *not* staying here. If you do not carry a moonstone, you will be subject to Fey justice."

Kenric stood up taller and met her hostile gaze. "I must see Cerinor and your king."

The Fey with the bow and arrow stalked over to Kenric's side. He had a clear bead on Hnagi. "Whatever you do with the human, I say let's kill the goblin now."

Kenric's heart began to gallop. "Would you kill a goblin who is under Cerinor's protection?"

Surprised, the Fey archer looked at Faroth and Linwe. Reluctantly, Linwe nodded. "It is true that Cerinor did not want him killed." She smiled, showing sharp little teeth. "But that was last time. He may have changed his mind since then." She studied the two humans and the goblin in front of her. "I say we split up. Half the patrol will guide the older human to the western edge of Grim Wood tonight. That way we shall be rid of him as soon as possible. The rest of us will take these two to Elga Mora."

Immediately, six guards encircled Kenric's father. "Go on," one of them said, nudging Brogan with the tip of his bow.

Brogan looked back at Kenric. "I will never forgive myself if you are harmed."

"I won't be," Kenric said, wishing he were more certain of this. The Fey's hostility was as thick as a stone wall, and just as impossible to break through.

Led by the Fey, his father turned and began his journey toward the western border. Kenric fought down the urge to run after him and give him one last hug goodbye. He was afraid the Fey would see it as a sign of weakness. Besides, if Linwe scorned him for it, he would have to punch her. His father wouldn't be pleased he hit a girl. Even if it was a rude, scornful Fey one.

Kenric turned his attention back to Linwe and Faroth. Linwe sheathed her dagger and pulled two strips of cloth from her belt. "Your goblin must be blindfolded. I will not touch goblin flesh, so you will have to do it."

Annoyed, Kenric took the strip of cloth from her hand. "It's not fair to blindfold him just because he's a goblin."

"Don't worry. We will blindfold you as well. No one may see the way to Elga Mora."

"What is Elga Mora, anyway?"

"The heart of Mithin Dûr, where the Fey dwell."

Kenric had forgotten the Fey had their own name for Grim Wood. He turned to Hnagi. "I have to wear one, too, if it makes you feel any better."

"Only thing make Hnagi feel better is getting firestone and going home," the goblin grumbled, but there wasn't much heat behind his words. Kenric tied the blindfold around Hnagi's eyes.

Linwe held out a length of vine. "Now bind his hands."

Kenric started to protest.

"Just as we will bind yours," she said.

Kenric wrapped the vine around Hnagi's wrists, careful not to make it too tight. Linwe reached out and took the goblin's dagger from his belt. She held it between two fingers, as if it might bite. One of the larger Fey stepped forward. He draped a rough sack over the goblin, then tossed him over his shoulder. Hnagi squealed once, then fell silent.

Next, Linwe and Faroth approached Kenric. They bound and blindfolded him, and were none too gentle about it. He felt Linwe lift his dagger from its sheath. Faroth grabbed Kenric around the middle, as if he were going to throw him over his shoulder.

"No! My feet and legs work fine. I will walk, not be lugged around like a sack of grain."

"Only if you can keep up," said Linwe. "If you slow us down, we will carry you."

"What are you always so mad about, anyway?" Kenric asked her.

Linwe sniffed. "You are not Fey. Therefore, you do not belong in the forest. Now walk." She put the tip of her dagger to his spine. Kenric walked.

⋈ 5 ⊱

Kenric stumbled blindly down a path he could not see. Tangled roots and bracken tripped him. Only Linwe's grip on his arm kept him from falling.

Kenric lost track of the hours as they marched. After a while, the ground under his feet became soft and springy. It felt as if he were walking on thick, new grass. He heard a brook burbling nearby. A gentle breeze ruffled his hair.

Finally, they stopped. The blindfold was removed and Kenric stood blinking in the midday light. He was shocked to discover they had walked all through the night and most of the morning. He was standing outside an enormous cluster of tall, silvery white trees.

"Elga Mora," Linwe said. "Something few humans have ever seen." She looked over at Hnagi in disgust.

"And no goblins, ever. Keep him blindfolded," she instructed.

Kenric couldn't be sure, but thought he heard Hnagi whimper.

It looked as if the Fey had coaxed the trees to grow together to form a huge dwelling. Tree trunks wider than Kenric's house grew upward into tall, graceful arches. Clusters of branches and leaves twisted together to form delicate rooftops and canopies.

"Quit your gawking," Linwe said with a little jab to his ribs.

She herded him through an archway into the circle of trees. Kenric expected it to be dark and gloomy inside, but it wasn't. The silver bark glowed faintly. He glanced upward at the thick tangle of leaves. Thin rays of sunlight trickled down and reflected off the bright leaves. The whole feeling was of green light and air.

Inside the enormous tree circle was a large clearing. The trunks were big enough to live in, which seemed to be what the Fey did. Small doors sat in the center of each trunk.

Farther in, Kenric saw more trees. These were slender and grew close enough together to form walls—walls made of trees. Kenric had never heard of such a thing. These walled areas seemed to be gathering places. They were filled with large numbers of Fey. Some were eating, others talking in groups. Small Fey—children, Kenric realized—were playing tag. When they caught sight of Kenric and Hnagi, the Fey stopped what they were doing. The musical rise and fall of their voices died away.

Faroth and Linwe ignored them and made their way to a second, slightly smaller circle of trees with another archway. Two guards stood in front of the opening. They wore tunics of silver mail and held wicked-looking silver spears in their hands.

Faroth stepped forward and whispered to them. With a scowl at Kenric, one of the guards slipped into the circle of trees. Kenric realized it was their version of a great hall. There was a dais in the front. A Fey with a golden beard sat on a large carved throne. Kenric realized he must be the king. A small group of older Fey stood behind him on the dais, talking among themselves.

The guard approached the king and whispered in his ear. The king nodded. The guard headed back to the archway where their small group waited. "We are to bring them before King Valorin," he told Faroth.

Linwe jabbed Kenric in the back. "Move."

Faroth led them through the crowd of Fey. As Kenric drew closer, he was able to get a better look at the Fey king. He was more polished-looking than the others. He had no twigs or leaves in his hair or beard, and his tunic was made of silver cloth. An enormous moonstone hung from a silver chain around his neck. But for all his splendor, something about him made Kenric uneasy. His face was thin and gaunt, as if his responsibilities ate away at him. There was a glint in his eye that spoke of an iron will and a quick temper.

The king studied Kenric. "What have you dragged in this time, Faroth? More vermin?"

"Aye, Your Majesty. But this vermin claims to carry a royal message."

The king narrowed his eyes. "And what is this *royal* message you carry?"

Kenric ignored the king's mocking tone. "I am Kenric of Penrith. I am sent by King Thorgil. He wants me to tell you that Mordig has been captured. His reign of evil is over."

A small murmur of surprise ran through the Fey in the room.

"But King Thorgil can only hold Mordig for a short while. He wishes that Fey and humans work together to find a way to permanently defeat Mordig. He is also looking for lore that tells how to forge a true blade of power, which he needs to destroy Mordig."

King Valorin's gray eyes glowed brightly as he took in Kenric's words. "It is good to hear that Mordig is dealt with. But know this, human. Just because you've taken care of this evil does not mean Fey and man are now allies. Mordig was a human problem."

Kenric stared in dismay. Surely the Fey king understood how dangerous Mordig was? "King Thorgil was hoping to form the alliances of old once more—"

"Bah! Too much has passed to call upon those alliances ever again. That time is over. This is a new age. Every race must fend for itself or be lost." The king lifted a silver goblet from the table beside the throne and drank from it.

Kenric stepped forward, trying to get the king's attention. A guard stopped him with his lowered spear. "But surely you wish to protect your people from Mordig?"

King Valorin set his goblet down so hard the contents sloshed over the side. "Silence! The ills that befall the land outside Mithin Dûr's borders have nothing to do with us."

The king's stubbornness had blinded him, Kenric realized.

"Do not come here claiming the Fey owe Thorgil anything," Valorin continued.

Out of the corner of his eye, Kenric saw Linwe shift uneasily.

A quiet anger began to simmer through Kenric. "But, Your Majesty, if you do not help, Mordig will swallow up the land of men."

King Valorin glared at Kenric. "Man's affairs do not concern me. I owe them nothing. In the Fey's darkest hour, they would not lift a finger to help us. Why should I help them now?"

Kenric tried to stay calm. "But, Your Majesty, what do you think Mordig will do when he's finished with us? Do you really think he'll leave you and your forest alone? Do you truly believe the Fey are safe from his plotting?"

"He would not dare!" Valorin said.

"Perhaps the boy is right," said an old Fey from the group of elders. Kenric saw it was Cerinor and felt a spark of hope. The last time he had tried to speak with the Fey, Cerinor had been the only one who had listened.

King Valorin frowned. "Why would you trust this human?"

"He and I have met before."

"Why was I not told of this?"

"Told of what, Your Majesty? That a traveler had been granted safe passage because of the moonstone he carried?" Cerinor continued. "Surely you do not wish to be interrupted every time someone passes through the woods?"

The king waved his hand. "No, that is true enough. But he has brought a goblin into our midst. How can you trust such a human?"

"But he is such a small goblin, Your Majesty. He could not possibly do any harm."

Valorin's eyes narrowed. "Show me this small goblin."

The Fey carrying Hnagi pulled the sack off his shoulder. He turned it upside down and dumped Hnagi out onto the floor. The little goblin huddled there as they pulled off the blindfold and untied his hands. At all the bright light, Hnagi quickly clamped them over his eyes, then peered out between his fingers.

King Valorin got up from his throne and came down the steps. He reached out and nudged Hnagi with the toe of his boot. Hnagi squeezed himself even smaller.

"Well, you are right. This goblin doesn't seem capable of hurting anyone."

Cerinor spoke quietly, his calm voice reminding Kenric of the one his father used with skittish horses. "I think we need to give this boy a chance. If what he says is true, then we owe it to our people."

One of the council members stepped forward. "My lord, what could it hurt to let the lad spend a day or two looking for answers? He is not asking the Fey to take up their swords on man's behalf quite yet. He is merely asking to search for answers in our lore."

Valorin threw an uneasy glance at the elders. All their eyes were fixed on him, waiting for his decision. "How can these things have anything to do with us? We are Fey. We are above the human world."

"Ripples in a pond, Your Majesty," Cerinor murmured. "Everything, even man and Fey, is connected in some small way."

King Valorin got a cunning gleam in his eye. Kenric didn't like it one bit. "How sure of this boy are you, Cerinor? Sure enough for a little friendly wager?"

Cerinor raised a bushy eyebrow. "A wager might be interesting."

"Very well. This boy and his goblin may have until the full moon to comb through our lore. I am certain he will find nothing of any use to him. If I'm right and he finds nothing, you must agree to remove yourself and your human-loving ways from the council."

Murmurs of astonishment ran through the room. That didn't sound like a friendly wager to Kenric. He had the feeling he'd just stepped into the middle of a very old argument between the two Fey.

Cerinor looked steadily into the king's eyes. "Is that what you truly want, Your Majesty? For me to resign from the council?"

The king hesitated, then he smiled, but there was no warmth to it. "Yes. That is a wager I will gladly make." He rubbed his hands and turned to Kenric. "You have until the full moon to make your case. If you are wrong, you will be declared outlaw of the Fey and banished from Mithin Dûr. If you ever set foot here again, your life is forfeit. Moonstone or no."

❈ 6 ❈

CERINOR CAME FORWARD and put his hand out to
Kenric. "So we meet again. I thought we might."

"You did?" Kenric asked.

Cerinor nodded. "Yes. Now, collect your goblin and
follow me. There is much to do, and we must get
started." The elder Fey turned to Faroth. "May I borrow
Linwe for the next three days, Captain?"

Faroth gave a small bow. "I'm sure she would be glad
to guard your prisoner for you."

Cerinor waved his hand. "No, no. He is not my prisoner. He is an honored guest."

A sour look passed between Linwe and Faroth.

Kenric turned his back on them and hurried over to

Hnagi, who still lay huddling on the floor. He knelt down beside him. "Are you all right?" he asked.

The goblin looked around uneasily. "Is nasty shouting Fey gone?"

"Shh! Yes, the king has left," Kenric said.

Hnagi pushed himself to his feet, his ears drooping. "Hnagi want to go home."

"Soon," Kenric promised.

"Come along now," Cerinor called out. "There is no time to waste."

"How long do we have until the full moon?" Kenric asked.

"Three days," Linwe said, then fell into place behind him. She started to lift her dagger to prod him, but he raised his eyebrows at her. "I'm an honored guest this time, remember?"

She huffed out a breath, sheathed her dagger, and began walking.

Cerinor motioned Kenric to his side. "This is fine news you bring, lad. Fine indeed. You deserve every Fey's thanks," he said, glancing meaningfully at Linwe.

"Well, I appreciate your thanks. But I'm worried

about what will happen if Mordig breaks out of the stone. The magic that holds him there is tied to the king and will only last as long as he lives. King Thorgil is old and fading, and Princess Tamaril disappeared when Mordig came to power. He had hoped that the Fey would join forces with him. At the very least, he needs to see if they know how to forge a blade of power to use against Mordig. If there is such a thing as a true blade of power, that is. King Thorgil thought he had one, but it didn't hold up to Mordig's attack. He says a true blade of power would have."

"We will ask Rindelorn. If there is ancient knowledge to be found, he will help us find it."

Cerinor led them to one of the giant tree trunks. He knocked on the small door in the center of it. "Come in," a voice called out. "I'll be with you in a moment."

Cerinor opened the door and motioned them inside. Kenric stepped into a room that was as small and snug as a rabbit's den. It would have been dark except for glowing globes placed in holders on the wall. Pale white light swirled inside them, as if they held moonlight itself.

Kenric turned from the globes and saw piles of rolled parchment teetering unsteadily on shelves. A large desk took up half the room. Dusty leather books filled every bookshelf. More were stacked in piles on the floor. An old wrinkled Fey sat at the desk.

The room was quiet except for the soft *scritch, scritch* of a quill on parchment.

"There," the wizened Fey said at last, putting aside his quill. He looked up, frowning when he saw Kenric and Hnagi. "What's all this about?" he asked in a gruff voice.

"Now, Rindelorn. Just hear us out before you get your whiskers in a knot," Cerinor said.

"But . . . but that's a goblin," Rindelorn spluttered.

"Oh, come now," Cerinor said impatiently. "I expected better of you. You're one of the few who can remember back to when goblins and Fey were on friendly terms. Now, let the boy explain."

Kenric wiped his damp palms on his pants and explained his task to Rindelorn.

"Well, you've come to the right place. Now, let me see, where would I have put blade lore?" The old Fey crossed to one of the bookshelves. He threw one last uneasy glance at Hnagi, then began searching. After a bit, he gave up and went over to a stack of dusty old scrolls. "Hmm. I don't seem to have anything on blades here. But something is tickling my memory." Rindelorn pursed his lips and stroked his chin. "I can't recall it now, but I'm sure it will come to me."

"Very well," Cerinor said. "What do you have on the old alliances? It wouldn't hurt to remind the king of that part of our history."

"All of that's been stored away in the archives for the last hundred years. I think everyone's forgotten it even exists."

"Maybe that's the problem," Cerinor said. "Can you take us to the archives?"

"We could take a trip down there," Rindelorn said. "It's time for a visit anyway. I haven't been down there in moons."

"Perfect," Cerinor said. "We shall go along and keep you company."

They followed Rindelorn into a small corridor. It quickly turned into a tunnel that led downward, twisting and turning. Kenric reached out and touched the wall.

"Glinden tree roots," Linwe explained. "The trees' roots act as passageways that lead to the bottom level of Elga Mora."

The root system twisted and turned so many times that Kenric lost count. After a while, he thought he heard footsteps behind them. He turned around to see who was following them, but no one was there.

"What's wrong?" Linwe asked, glancing over her shoulder.

"Nothing," Kenric said.

They marched along inside the hollowed-out root until they reached a tangled mass of smaller roots that barred their way. Rindelorn mumbled something in the strange, musical Fey tongue. There was a rustling noise and the roots pulled back to make an opening. Rindelorn motioned them all inside. After the last of them passed through, the roots twisted closed again.

The archives were an enormous room with hollows carved into the walls. Like a honeycomb, Kenric thought. The hollows were stuffed full of more scrolls, books, and parchments than Kenric could ever have imagined.

"This may take a while," Cerinor said.

"Well, the sooner we begin, the sooner we will have answers. You look over there in the Beginning of Time section. I'll search over here for blade lore." Rindelorn grabbed a parchment, took a seat, and began reading. Cerinor did the same.

Kenric reached out and plucked a scroll from one of the hollows. He laid it on the table beside him. When he went to sit down, however, the scroll was gone.

He looked up and saw Linwe clutching the scroll in her arms. "I'll search this one."

"All right," Kenric said. He didn't care which scroll he read as long as they found what they were looking for.

He got up and pulled another scroll out of the same honeycomb and placed it on the table. As he sat down, Linwe craned her head around to read the title. "*A Brief History of the Goblin Wars.* I think I should read this one as well." She reached out and snatched it off the table.

Kenric frowned at her, annoyed. His hands itched to grab the scroll back, but he didn't want to play tug-of-war with ancient Fey lore.

He got up and found another scroll. Before he could sit down again, Linwe called over to Rindelorn. "Do you think it's right to let him see our sacred lore?"

Rindelorn looked up from the book he was reading. "That's a good question. Maybe—"

"Enough," Cerinor growled. Rindelorn fell silent and turned back to his book.

"I was just checking," Linwe muttered. "And what about the goblin?"

Cowering next to Kenric, Hnagi spoke up. "Hnagi not know scratchings on paper."

"You mean you can't read?" Kenric asked.

Hnagi shook his head.

"That's just as well," Cerinor said. "Otherwise we would have another argument."

Kenric shook his head. He didn't understand how the elder Fey could be so good-natured about Linwe's grumpiness. It made Kenric want to smack her.

He pushed that thought out of his mind and unrolled the scroll. He opened it, dismayed to see unfamiliar markings on the page. He couldn't make out a word.

"Can't you read?" asked Linwe.

"Yes, I can read! Just not this." He turned to Cerinor. "What type of writing is this?"

"Fey runes," Cerinor said, coming to stand next to him.

Kenric looked back at the strange markings on the paper. "If you show me what the runes for *Fey, man,* and *goblin* look like, then I can mark those passages for you to read later."

"Very good. Here." Cerinor drew the symbols in the dust with one bony finger.

Kenric nodded. Ignoring Linwe, he turned to his scroll.

With her arms full of the things she'd grabbed from Kenric, Linwe sat down at the other end of the table and began to read.

Kenric tried to concentrate on the complex writing in front of him, but he couldn't. The hairs on the back of his neck twitched and stirred, making him jumpy. Certain that Linwe must be staring at him, he looked up. Her eyes were fixed on the page in front of her. Kenric quickly glanced around the room. Everyone was focused on their task, except Hnagi. He was curled up at Kenric's feet with his eyes closed.

"Hah!" Rindelorn called out, making Kenric jump. "*'The hand of man and the hand of Fey, linked together will forge the way,'*" he read.

The words hung in the musty air of the archives.

"That's it!" said Kenric.

"That doesn't prove anything!" said Linwe.

"Is there any more?" Cerinor asked.

Rindelorn looked at the parchment. "I'm afraid not. That's the last bit on this scroll."

He put the scroll aside and picked up the next one, scanning rapidly. He sighed and shook his head. "No, there is no more mention of Fey and man working together."

Just then, there was a loud *thud* as something hit the archive door.

7

KENRIC LEAPED TO HIS FEET and rushed to the doorway. Linwe was right on his heels. He knew something had been following them! He tried to push past the tangled mass of roots, but they held firm. He heard Linwe mutter something in the Fey tongue and the roots parted.

Kenric saw nothing as he stumbled into the hallway. Then a shrill, chattering screech exploded just above his head. Something launched itself straight at him. He ducked. There was a small thud against his chest, and the sharp prick of tiny claws. Kenric looked down into two huge brown eyes in a furry, pointed face. It was an animal of some kind.

Kenric struggled to untangle the claws stuck in his

shirt. No sooner were they free than the creature scrambled up Kenric's arm to his shoulder. Then it wrapped itself around his neck.

"Dulcet!" Linwe said. "What are you doing here?" She reached out to take the creature off Kenric's shoulder. The little animal squealed and chattered and held fast to Kenric.

Kenric felt as if he'd won a small victory. A Fey creature preferred him over Linwe!

"Dulcet seems to have taken a liking to you." Linwe put her hands on her hips and frowned at the creature. "She normally has more sense than that."

This must be what he had sensed following them in the tunnels, Kenric realized. The creature looked like a cross between a fox and a squirrel. "What is it?" he asked.

"My favorite pet. A hilfen," Linwe said. "Very dangerous, this hilfen. Especially if you're a gildaberry."

Rindelorn came forward. "Away with you! I can't concentrate with all this noise."

"It's getting late anyway," Cerinor said. "I'm sure some of us are tired and hungry."

With one last frown at the goblin, Rindelorn bid them good night.

Cerinor smiled. "He is like a fox, that one. Now that he has scented his prey, he won't give up until the knowledge is safely in his hands. Come along, then."

Kenric put a hand up to make sure the hilfen was secure, then followed Cerinor through the tunnels. They passed a small group of Fey who stopped talking to stare at them. Linwe scowled, but Cerinor ignored them. When they reached the main hallway, the few Fey gathered there crossed to the other side.

With a start, Kenric realized Linwe and Cerinor were being shunned.

"I think it might be best if we dined in my chambers this evening," Cerinor said, his voice low.

Kenric imagined an entire evening with Linwe scowling at him. "Um, I'd hate to keep Linwe away from her other duties too long," he said.

Linwe knew immediately what he was up to. "I don't want to eat with you, either," she said. "But I can't be your guard if I'm not near you."

"But I'm an honored guest, remember? I don't need a guard."

Linwe's eyes narrowed at his challenge, and her hand went to her dagger.

"Linwe!" Cerinor scolded her. "If you cannot keep your temper in check, perhaps you should leave."

Linwe opened her mouth to argue, but Cerinor shook his head. "No. That is all for tonight. We will see you in the morning, if you have found your manners by then."

With flushed cheeks, Linwe whirled around and left without a word. Both Cerinor and Kenric stared after her.

"She'll be calmer tomorrow, after she's had a chance to sleep," Cerinor said.

"I don't think so." Kenric gently moved the hilfen's tail away from his mouth. "She seems pretty sure of her hatred."

"Linwe is merely clinging to her anger because it is safe. Her mind is quick, and she senses the truth in your words. But it threatens everything she has ever known. Having your world turned upside down is not pleasant."

Kenric knew this was true. He remembered clearly how confused and upset he had been when his father had disappeared. The whole world had looked black then.

"She is willing you to be wrong, to fail in your task. But in her heart," Cerinor continued, "she knows you are right, and I'm sure that she'll help you succeed."

8

CERINOR'S QUARTERS WERE like Rindelorn's, only a little bigger and less cluttered. Dinner was quiet. Both Kenric and Cerinor chewed on their thoughts as much as on their food. Hnagi grumbled at the lack of raw meat. He spent the rest of the evening eyeing Dulcet hungrily.

When the meal was over, the elder Fey showed Kenric to a spare room. It was small and the shelves were lined with books and scrolls. There was a moon globe on a small table and a hollowed-out nook in the wall for sleeping.

Exhausted, Kenric climbed into the sleeping hollow, surprised at how comfortable it was. Dulcet scrambled up next to him. He was half afraid the goblin was going to hop into bed with them as well, but he stayed on the floor.

"Are you going to be warm enough down there?" Kenric asked.

Hnagi sniffed and turned his back to Kenric. "Hnagi fine."

With a frustrated sigh, Kenric flopped back on his bed. A cranky goblin was the least of his worries.

Kenric's thoughts turned to the three days he'd been given. That wasn't very much time. Not for all the answers he had to find. If he failed, they would have no chance against Mordig when he finally broke free of the stone. And King Thorgil was certain he would, eventually. How could he face his king if he failed? Pushing that disturbing thought aside, he fell into a troubled sleep.

SOMETHING WOKE HIM. The moon globe still glowed, but its light just barely pierced the darkness. Kenric blinked to clear the sleep from his eyes. A snuffling sound reached his ears.

Kenric leaned over and looked down at the floor. Hnagi sat in a heap, sniffling.

"Are you okay?"

"Oh, yes. Hnagi fine. Nasty Fey everywhere. Want to cut Hnagi's throat."

"I tried to warn you," Kenric said.

Hnagi took a deep, snuffling sigh. "Ken-ric not want Hnagi anymore. Fur-face more fun."

The goblin was jealous! Thanks to Kenric, Hnagi was stuck somewhere where everyone hated him. Now the goblin was afraid he'd been replaced by a cute new pet. No wonder poor Hnagi felt abandoned and alone.

"Hnagi, she's just Linwe's pet. I don't even know why she likes me so much. She's not my friend, like you are," Kenric whispered.

Hnagi's ugly little face brightened. "Really?"

"Really," Kenric said. He opened his mouth to say more, but was cut off by a *whoosh* that raced across his back, followed by *whoosh, whoosh.*

There was a prickle along his spine. Dulcet squealed, then leaped off the bed. She ran across the floor and disappeared from view.

"What was that?" Hnagi asked.

Dread seeped into his bones, and Kenric was almost afraid to turn around. "I don't know," he whispered, his throat suddenly dry. He was tempted to dive for the floor like Dulcet had, but he needed to know what had caused that sound.

Slowly he eased back up onto the bed and turned around. In the darkness, he could just make out three arrows quivering in the wall behind him.

His muscles grew wobbly and all the air left his lungs.

The arrows had passed just inches above his back. If he had been lying in bed instead of leaning over the side, they would have pierced his ribs.

He quickly rolled off the bed onto the floor. He thought about looking for Cerinor, but he would be a clear target as he headed for the door. And he didn't know where the old Fey's sleeping chamber was. The idea of stumbling around in the dark while dodging arrows seemed unwise.

Heart thudding, he knelt beside Hnagi and whispered, "Come on. Let's go over there, under the table."

Trembling, Hnagi scuttled on all fours over to the table. Kenric tried to peer into the darkness, but could see nothing. He took a deep breath, hoping it wouldn't be his last. Then he hurried across the floor.

Kenric scooted so that his back was against the wall. He wasn't sure where the arrows had come from, but the table would give them some protection. Hnagi curled up against his left side. After a few moments, Dulcet crawled out of her hiding place and draped herself across Kenric's neck.

Soon, the goblin was breathing steadily, sending reeking carrion breath in Kenric's direction. Dulcet began to purr. The rumble of her little chest was soft and steady. It gave Kenric something to listen to throughout the long, sleepless night.

THE THREE OF THEM stayed huddled under the table until morning. When Kenric couldn't bear his cramped muscles a moment longer, he stretched. Hnagi clacked his teeth in his sleep, then woke with a start. Dulcet opened one big eye, then tried to go back to sleep. As Kenric stood up, she scolded him and slipped off his shoulder.

Kenric forced himself to walk over to the bed. He reached out and touched one of the arrows. It was made of some hard black wood and fletched with black feathers. Raven perhaps. As he touched it, Dulcet screeched loudly, then ran toward the door.

"It's okay," he murmured, embarrassed to find that his voice shook.

"Tell fur-face hush! Make Hnagi head ache!" Hnagi

said. He came over to the bed, then whimpered when he saw the arrows. "Nasty Fey! Nasty, nasty Fey," he said.

Kenric didn't correct him. "I need to tell Cerinor." And Linwe, he thought. Although she'd probably be sorry the arrows had missed.

The elder Fey was where Kenric had left him last night. He sat bent over a scroll. Many more littered his desk. "Have you stayed up all night?" Kenric asked.

Cerinor looked up. "Eh? I suppose I have." He looked back down at the scrolls. "All this history is fascinating. How did you sleep?"

"Not very well. I had a visitor." Kenric held up one of the black arrows.

Cerinor jerked his head up and narrowed his eyes. "Where did that come from?"

Kenric led Cerinor into his room and pointed to the bed.

Cerinor's eyebrows shot up. He hurried over to the bed to examine the other arrows. "Assassin's arrows," he announced grimly.

Hnagi's grip on Kenric grew so tight it pinched.

"Which means that someone has ignored that you've been placed under my protection." The Fey's face grew terrible in his anger. Kenric drew back without thinking.

"Or . . ." Cerinor paused, as if he were thinking. "Or the king has removed his protection."

There was a knock at the door.

"Hopefully, that's Linwe." Cerinor hurried to the door. Linwe came in, already fuming. "That traitor Dulcet stayed here last night, didn't she?" she said to Cerinor.

Ignoring her question, the elder Fey explained what had happened during the night.

"Assassin's arrows!" Linwe repeated, nearly shouting. "Let me see."

She pushed into the room, her eyes zeroing in on the bed. Barely glancing at Kenric, she asked, "Were you hit?"

Kenric shook his head.

"And what of the goblin? Was he hurt?" she asked as she knelt to examine the arrows.

Was that a hopeful note in her voice? Kenric wondered. "No. And his name is Hnagi. You might try using it sometime."

She ignored him and stood up. "From now on, I shall be your bodyguard," she said. "You have been given Fey protection. As a point of honor I must see that you stay safe."

"I thought you were already guarding me," Kenric said.

Linwe snorted. "No. I was making sure you would do nothing to hurt the Fey. But now it seems I must protect you from them."

"How annoying for you," Kenric muttered.

Linwe scowled at him, then turned to Cerinor. "Should we report this to the king?"

Slowly, Cerinor shook his head. "No. Not until we have a better idea of who's behind it."

Linwe gasped, then her face grew pale. "You don't think . . . ?

"I mean I don't know who is behind this, and it is best not to tip our hand too soon. Now come. We have much to do this morning, and our time is running short. Let us go visit the smiths."

❈ 9 ❈

THEY MADE THEIR WAY through the root tunnels to the smiths' forge. Much to Kenric's surprise, the forge was inside one of the giant trees. Kenric watched a smith shove a piece of metal into the fire. "Aren't you afraid the fire will burn down your tree?" he asked Cerinor.

The old Fey smiled. "Not at all. It is cold fire, you see."

"Cold fire?" Kenric repeated.

"Moon fire," Linwe said, impatiently. "It burns cold and will not harm the tree."

One of the smiths bowed to Cerinor, then handed his tongs to a smaller smith. An apprentice, Kenric thought, like himself.

"Marolas"—Cerinor greeted the smith who came over to them—"I want you to meet Kenric. He has come on a mission for his king. We thought perhaps you could help us."

Marolas looked Kenric up and down. "I heard there was a human in Elga Mora," he said at last. His voice wasn't friendly.

"A goblin, too," he continued. He peered around Kenric to have a look at Hnagi, who tried to hide behind Kenric's leg. "What do you need from a simple smith like myself?"

Cerinor nodded at Kenric. "I will let Kenric tell you."

So Kenric told Marolas of Mordig. He told of imprisoning the evil lord in the stone, and of the blade Mordig had been trying to make. Marolas's eyes widened in surprise as Kenric described the sword's disappearance. Lastly, Kenric told the smith about the blade of power that King Thorgil wanted to forge. The smith looked thoughtful.

Then Linwe spoke and broke the spell. "Cerinor and the human believe that the answer is for humans and Fey to work together to forge this blade."

Marolas threw back his head and laughed. "Fey and man? Working together? You're as bad as old Thulidor!"

Kenric's pulse quickened. "Thulidor? Who is he? Does he talk of the humans and Fey working together?"

"Used to. Used to believe in the old stories his grand-father had told him."

Kenric took a step forward. "Can I speak with him? I want to hear these old stories for myself."

Marolas shrugged. "Thulidor no longer lives here in Mithin Dûr."

"Where is he, then?" Kenric asked as Cerinor frowned in thought.

"Five years ago he quit the forge and traveled to Aryn Dûr. He decided to wait there for his final journey across the Silver Sea."

"I always wondered why he left so soon," Cerinor said. "Perhaps it is time to find out."

Marolas shook his head. "It was nothing more than a foolish old Fey's prattle. He was always rambling on about something. The land would not be healed until all three races joined forces, things like that. He even claimed that he had access to some treasure of the human race."

Kenric froze. "Human treasure? Did he say what it was?"

"No, he didn't. Why do you ask?" Marolas said with suspicion.

Ignoring the smith, Kenric thought furiously. He had

not told Cerinor or Linwe about his search for Princess Tamaril. Perhaps it was time he did.

Cerinor threw a sharp glance at Kenric. "Well, he is a human after all. It makes sense he would be interested in human treasures. Thank you for your time. You have given us something, at least," he said.

Marolas glanced at Hnagi again, then spit into the fire. "I wasn't trying to."

Ignoring the smith, Cerinor motioned the others out of the forge. Once they were out of hearing range, he turned to Kenric. "What did Marolas's words mean to you? And they do mean something. I saw it in your eyes."

Kenric cleared his throat. "They do mean something, yes. One of the things I am supposed to do while I'm in Grim Wood is look for the king's daughter. Princess Tamaril escaped when Mordig came to power. We think she came to Grim Wood."

Linwe interrupted with a scoff. "There is no runaway princess here."

Kenric looked up and met Linwe's eyes. "King Thorgil thinks the bloodstone you found was hers."

"How can that be?" she spluttered. "Surely we would know of such a thing."

"She must have come to Grim Wood like the king told her to. Then perhaps she lost the stone once she was here."

"The ripples in the pond reach farther than I thought," Cerinor said. He grew silent then, staring off into space, deep in thought.

"Where did you find the bloodstone, Linwe?" Kenric asked.

"On the eastern edge of Mithin Dûr. Halfway between the Old Road and the ward stone."

"And you saw no sign of anyone? Nothing to show who might have dropped it?"

"No," Linwe said. "There were signs that someone had come through the forest recently. But no hint of who they were or why."

It wasn't much to go on. "How long ago did you find it?"

"Nearly five years ago." Linwe's eyes widened as she realized what she'd said.

Kenric nodded. "Five years ago is when Tamaril had to leave Tirga Mor."

Cerinor narrowed his eyes. "Which is also the time Thulidor took it in his head to retire to Aryn Dûr. Hmm."

"Marolas did not say Thulidor had made the trip to

Dûr Haven, yet," Linwe said. "I think we should go to Aryn Dûr to find him."

"What exactly is Aryn Dûr?" Kenric asked.

"It is a small Fey village in the north of Mithin Dûr," Cerinor told him. "It is where Fey go to await their final trip across the Silver Sea." The elder Fey turned back to Linwe. "We will pay my old friend a visit, feyling, but not yet. For now, we'll return to the archives and see what Rindelorn may have found."

MUCH LATER, their small group sat in Cerinor's chambers. It had been a long day of searching and finding nothing. Kenric was discouraged and hungry.

He perked up at the knock on the door.

"Dinner," Cerinor announced. He opened the door, and two Fey servants came in bearing heavy trays. Cerinor hastily cleared a spot on his desk.

The Fey set the trays down. They cast quick, furtive glances at Hnagi, then looked at Linwe. "Will you be dining here, Princess?" The servant lowered his voice. "With a goblin?"

Linwe stuck her chin out, and her eyes snapped. "I will dine where I please."

"Yes, but . . ." the servant's words trailed off as he looked at Hnagi again.

Cerinor frowned at them. "You are dismissed," he said sternly.

Confused, the servants disappeared with one last curious glance over their shoulders.

"Princess?" Kenric repeated.

"Yes," Cerinor said. "Linwe is King Valorin's daughter and heir to the throne."

Linwe glanced uneasily at Kenric, her cheeks flushed. "You can quit staring!" she said. "It changes nothing."

Kenric closed his mouth with a snap. She was embarrassed about being a princess. He worked to keep the smile off his face. It would take him a while to get used to that idea.

"What's for dinner?" Linwe asked, trying to change the subject. "I'm starving."

"Come," Cerinor said. "Let's eat and we will do our best to forget you're a princess."

Kenric stepped over the goblin and headed toward the table. "Come on, Hnagi."

The goblin followed him to the tray, then shook his

head. "Hnagi not like yucky Fey food." His eyes went immediately to Dulcet.

Kenric did not like the gleam in his eye. "Well, just make do with this for now, and tomorrow you can go out hunting."

With a heavy sigh, Hnagi lifted a piece of roasted meat from the tray. Then he went over to the fire and began gnawing.

Kenric piled his plate high with food.

Cerinor took a sip from his silver goblet, then set it down. "This is going more slowly than I had hoped. It's been one full day, and we have nothing to show for it. At this rate, I'll soon be off the council, and Kenric will be escorted out of Mithin Dûr."

"I still think we should go to Aryn Dûr," Linwe put in.

"Do we have time for that?" Kenric asked. "Can we get there and back in the two days we have left?"

"Even if we could, I am not sure how much good it will do," Cerinor said. "The king has grown most stubborn lately. He used to listen to reason. But now . . ." The elder Fey's words trailed off.

"Father has reasons for his bitterness and anger," Linwe said.

"Yes, but it is time to put them aside," Cerinor said. "Too much is at stake."

Kenric leaned forward. "What reasons? Why is he so bitter? If the Fey don't join forces with King Thorgil, their lives may be at risk. What is worth that?"

Linwe sucked in a breath. "You would dare to question a king?"

"It is his right to know, feyling," Cerinor said sharply. "If Valorin refuses to help Kenric's people, then he should know the reason why."

The elder Fey took a deep breath and settled back in his chair. "Once, a long time ago, when my father was but a boy, a terrible heartbreak befell the Fey. There was a princess whose grace and beauty spoke to the hearts of our people. She was named Marílla, but everyone called her the Heart of Mithin Dûr, so beloved was she."

"She was my great-grandmother," Linwe added, her face set in grim lines.

"One day, as Marílla strolled through the forests of Mithin Dûr, a goblin war party entered the woods. Keep in mind, we were not at odds with the goblins then. They were, in fact, our allies."

Linwe gasped. "You have said that twice now! My father never mentioned that."

"After a while, it doesn't matter if a story is truthful anymore. Especially when its only purpose is to stoke the fires of hatred." Cerinor turned back to Kenric. "This war party had but one goal—to capture the princess Marílla, to steal the Heart of Mithin Dûr. Which they did."

"Why?" asked Kenric.

Cerinor shrugged. "We did not know then. We do not know now."

Hnagi shrank closer to Kenric's knee. "Do you know why?" Kenric asked him.

Hnagi shook his head so fiercely that his ears flapped.

Cerinor continued. "When the princess was taken, the sun disappeared for days. Even the trees drooped in sorrow. Of course, the Fey mounted a war party to bring her back. But she was never found. The Fey king tried to persuade the humans to join forces with him. He wanted to launch a full-scale war on the goblins. But the human king refused. He said the goblin king had sworn to him that they had nothing to do with the princess's disappearance. The goblins claimed it was a rogue warlord acting on his own. The human king believed him. The Fey king did not. We have never forgiven the humans for that."

Another silence fell over the room. Finally, Cerinor spoke. "As long as Mordig's evil has not touched the Fey, Valorin will not become involved. He is determined to keep the Fey out of the affairs of man."

At Cerinor's words, Linwe pushed her plate away. She looked as if she were about to throw herself off a cliff. "It's not true," she said softly.

All eyes at the table turned to her. "What is not true, feyling?" Cerinor asked.

"That the evil has not touched the Fey."

"Tell us!" Cerinor said.

"I cannot," Linwe said in a small voice. "My father swore the patrol to secrecy." She looked up at the elder, her eyes pleading. "He said he would take care of it. But he hasn't."

Kenric could feel her distress. Her father had asked her to lie for him. Kenric was sure his father would never do such a thing.

Cerinor grabbed Linwe's hand. "If it affects the Fey, the council needs to know."

Linwe took a deep breath. "The glinden trees on the eastern edges of the forest have begun to rot."

Cerinor's eyes blazed. "Rot? How? Nothing in Mithin Dûr rots." He sounded indignant at the very idea.

"The leaves turn brown and drop off the tree. The bark is no longer silver, but tainted with some ugly growth."

Kenric sat forward on his chair. Now maybe the Fey would believe him.

"How long ago did you discover this?" Cerinor demanded.

"Eight, nine moons ago. The patrol noticed it and immediately reported it to the king."

"Was it after your father had already begun to act strangely?" Cerinor's voice was gentle.

Linwe nodded, miserable.

"There must be some connection," Cerinor mused aloud, and leaned back in his chair. "Very well. You will show us these rotting glinden trees first thing in the morning."

☄ IO ☄

LINWE WAS WAITING for them at first light. She seemed quiet. Kenric wondered if she felt guilty for keeping the tree rot a secret for so long.

As soon as he stepped out of Cerinor's chamber, she moved to stand next to him. She was taking this bodyguard thing very seriously.

Outside, early-morning mist clung to the trees. Kenric could hear the steady *drip, drip, drip* of the morning dew as it slid off the leaves. In spite of the sunlight, he glanced over his shoulder, looking for shadows.

As they moved deeper into the forest, Dulcet leaped from Kenric's shoulder and scampered up the nearest tree. She ran ahead, then doubled back, keeping up a steady stream of playful chatter.

"What have you been feeding her?" Linwe asked. She held her hand out and clicked her tongue, trying to get Dulcet's attention.

"Whatever she snatches off my plate." Kenric grinned, trying to cheer Linwe up.

It didn't work. Especially since Dulcet wouldn't come to her. Linwe folded her arms across her chest and walked with her head down. She walked like that for the rest of the morning.

When it was almost noon, Cerinor finally asked, "Where exactly did you see this rot?"

"It was halfway between Elga Mora and the ward stone," Linwe said. "We'll be there in another hour."

"What's the ward stone?" Kenric asked, remembering they had mentioned it yesterday.

"Don't they teach you humans anything?" Linwe muttered.

Cerinor spoke up. "The ward stone is a stone memorial built where all three realms meet. It is made of—"

Linwe gasped. Kenric and Cerinor looked up to see what was wrong.

She pointed to the nearest tree. Its normally bright trunk was turning brown. "The rot hadn't come nearly this far last time I was here," Linwe said. She picked up her pace and hurried forward until, with a startled cry, she came to a stop.

Rotting trees stretched out before them as far as the eye could see. The once brilliant green leaves hung, brown and rotting in the sunlight. The branches drooped wearily, no longer able to hold up their weight. An ugly black-and-green mold began at the base of the trunks and spread upward. Some of the trees were nothing more than withered black trunks.

Dulcet squealed and leaped from an overhead branch directly into Kenric's arms.

"By the moon!" Cerinor exclaimed as he pushed forward to stare at the trees. "I have never seen such a thing."

"It's grown worse!" Linwe said, shaking her head in disbelief. "Could it be some illness that trees get from time to time?" she asked. "That's what father told us."

"No," said Cerinor. "This reeks of evil and therefore of Mordig."

"Well, King Valorin can't pretend the evil isn't in Mithin Dûr," Kenric said. "Not with this happening."

"And yet he has," Cerinor said, puzzled. "I can't imagine why he has hidden this from the council. Something is not right." His face grew hard. "Come, we must see how far back this goes."

They worked their way through the trees. The limp, rotting trunks and branches weighed heavily on everyone. It was as if they gave off some terrible mist or fog that pushed the mind to grim thoughts.

Up in front, Cerinor gave a shout, then rushed forward. Kenric hurried to catch up. A stream lay before them. But this was not a cheerful, bubbling stream. It was a dark, sludgy mess, full of fetid moss and stagnant mud. Small, round, white fish floated belly-up in the murk.

Dulcet took one look, then turned to burrow down the neck of Kenric's tunic.

"They have fouled our streams!" Linwe said, shocked. "Killed our moonfish!"

Kenric knelt beside the pool and dipped his fingers in the water. Immediately his fingers burned, then grew numb. He lifted his fingers and sniffed. They smelled of rot and decay.

Cerinor pulled him back. "Best not to touch it. We do not know the nature of this mess."

"Where is the stream's source?" Kenric asked. "Do we know where it flows from?"

Cerinor pursed his lips. "It must start somewhere up near Helgor's Teeth in the goblin realm. But I'd have to check one of Rindelorn's maps to be certain."

Linwe whirled to face Hnagi, her hand on her dagger. "This must be the goblins' doing!"

Hnagi squeaked and ducked behind Kenric.

"Hush, feyling. You will not fix things by bullying the goblin," Cerinor said. "This is much more powerful than anything they could do."

"Mordig," Kenric said.

"But why?" Linwe asked. "Why would he want to destroy our forest?"

"It is easier to conquer a weakened race than a strong one," Cerinor said. "We must speak to the king at once. Surely he will listen to us now."

WHEN THEY REACHED Elga Mora, they headed for the throne room. On their way, a voice called out to them. "Cerinor! I've been looking for you all day. I think I've found something."

They stopped and waited for Rindelorn to reach them.

"I would like to see what you've found," Cerinor said. "But first, we have urgent news for the king. Come with us. You should hear this as well."

The throne room was empty. Cerinor led them to the king's chambers, just behind the throne room. He knocked, and the king bade him enter.

King Valorin's eyes widened in surprise when he saw their small group. He put his quill down and leaned back in his chair. "A visit. How lovely." His eyes were sharp and wary.

Kenric waited while Cerinor explained what they'd seen. At his side, Linwe fidgeted and avoided meeting her father's eyes.

When Cerinor had finished talking, the king turned to Linwe. "You broke your promise to me! You'd agreed to keep silent."

Linwe flinched, but held her head high. "You always told me that my duty is to my people, not to my own desires. I wanted to do what you asked, but I had to think of all the Fey. The rot is growing worse, Father! More trees are dying. And it's not just the trees anymore. The poison has spread. It's fouling the streams and killing the fish."

King Valorin turned away.

She took a timid step forward. "Isn't it our duty to try to fix this?" There was a desperate note in her voice. "Would you have me lie to a member of the high council?"

"You should have told the council immediately," Cerinor said. "Not waited and hoped it would go away. Just how long did you plan to hide this from us? Do you have any idea how soon the streams will carry this rot into Elga Mora?"

"It is not your right to question your king," Valorin snapped. "I have told you that I am taking care of it. I do not have to explain my actions to you. Now leave!" He strode over to the door and threw it open.

As Cerinor passed through the door, he turned and met the king's eyes. "We will discuss this at tonight's moon feast."

They all walked through the main hallway in silence. No one knew what to say about the king's outburst. Linwe looked pale and stricken. "What is the moon feast?" Kenric finally asked, trying to take her mind off the king's harsh words.

"It's our most sacred festival," Linwe said. "At every full moon, we celebrate the gifts the moon has given us.

We have a feast, then gather at the lunila tree for our ceremony."

Linwe turned to him. "You should feel honored to attend the feast. There's never been a human at one in my lifetime. And certainly not a goblin."

❧ II ❧

Kenric had never seen anything so grand in all his life. The throne room had been turned into a banquet hall for the occasion. The pale tree trunks glowed with moonlight. The room was crowded with Fey of every age, from young children to wizened elders. Kenric would never have guessed that this many Fey existed in all the world.

They were decked out in all their finery. Crowns of leaves and flowers were woven into their hair. Feathers and moonstones decorated their gowns. Some of the men wore silver chain mail. Along the walls, delicate glass globes shimmered with pale light. The tables were piled high with every kind of food imaginable. Silver goblets held a honey-sweet drink that tickled Kenric's nose when he drank it.

He sat next to Cerinor, two tables over from the king. He was so busy taking in all the sights and eating and drinking his fill that he barely noticed the Fey's suspicious looks or pointed glances. Dulcet sat on his shoulder, eyeing a piece of yellow fruit on his plate. Glancing around to make sure no one was watching, Kenric slipped a piece of it to her. She chittered her thanks, then leaped off his shoulder and scurried away.

Hnagi sat quietly at Kenric's side, munching on a rib bone.

When at last the feast was over, the king stood. "Come," he announced. "It is time for the ceremony." He turned and looked at Kenric. "You must entertain yourself for the rest of the evening. Humans are not allowed to witness our moon ceremony."

Kenric stood. "I understand. I appreciate all the hospitality you have shown me so far."

The king nodded, then left the room. The Fey stood and followed him. Cerinor stopped with a worried frown. "You will be all right by yourself? Rindelorn is hot on the trail of some bit of lore. He didn't come to the feast and said he'd miss the ceremony as well. If you need anything, he's down in the archives."

"I should be fine," Kenric said. Truthfully, he was looking forward to a few hours alone.

Back in Cerinor's chambers, Kenric tried to sort out his thoughts. The Fey did not welcome outsiders. Nor did they want to renew the old alliance. For some reason, they believed nothing could touch them here in Mithin Dûr. If they didn't do something soon, they would lose their entire kingdom to the rot.

And Kenric had only one more day to prove it to them.

When the king had been given proof that Mordig's evil was tainting his land, he ignored it. He pretended it wasn't happening. Why? No matter how many different ways Kenric looked at the puzzle, he couldn't answer that one question. Either the king was refusing to see what was before his nose, or . . . or something much worse was going on.

Suddenly, he remembered Rindelorn. Just before they spoke to the king about the tree rot, Rindelorn had come looking for them. They'd all been so distracted by the rot that they'd never learned what he'd found.

"Come on, Hnagi," he said. "Let's go visit Rindelorn down in the archives. He might have some new information for us."

Dulcet scampered up Kenric's arm to his shoulder, not wanting to be left behind.

❧ 12 ❧

THE ROOTS THAT SEALED the archives were open slightly. Kenric called out, "Hello?" then stepped through the doorway. "Rindelorn?" Kenric's voice faltered at the deep silence.

Hnagi clutched Kenric's knee. "Hnagi not like this," the goblin whispered.

"Kenric doesn't either." He took two steps into the archives, then froze. A lump of fear rose up in his throat.

Rindelorn lay crumpled on the floor. A black arrow pierced his gut.

"No!" Kenric rushed forward and knelt beside the Fey. "No, no, no!" Kenric murmured, as if the words might undo the evil that had been done.

Rindelorn moaned. Kenric placed his hand on the old Fey's arm. "Don't move," he said. "We'll find help."

Kenric looked down at the wound. Whitish green liquid seeped out around the arrow. It took him a moment to realize Rindelorn was bleeding. The whitish green liquid was Fey blood!

"Hnagi, we need to find something to use for bandages," he called over his shoulder.

Kenric found a small cushion from one of the chairs to lay under Rindelorn's head. There were no blankets, so Kenric took off his outer tunic. As he laid it across the old Fey, he noticed a rumpled piece of paper in Rindelorn's hand. There was an open book on the floor next to him. Pages had been ripped out.

Kenric gently pried the crumpled page out of the old Fey's hand. He unfolded the piece of paper. It was in Fey runes. He couldn't read a word.

"Here." Hnagi's voice pulled Kenric's attention away from the paper. The goblin handed a piece of a shredded wall hanging to Kenric. Kenric carefully laid the soft material all around the wound, trying not to press too hard or touch the arrow.

He looked up at the goblin. "Can you stay here and keep an eye on him while I go and get the others?"

The goblin shivered and shrank under the desk. "What if more black arrows come?"

"I don't think they will." Kenric glanced at the torn book beside Rindelorn. "I think they got what they came for."

"What if other Fey come? Find Hnagi. Fey not like Hnagi." The goblin's eyes grew big.

He was right, Kenric realized. If the Fey discovered him, they would immediately think the goblin had done this.

"Well, you won't be any safer wandering around in Grim Wood, will you?"

Hnagi shuddered. "Hnagi stay here," he muttered.

"I'll hurry as fast as I can," Kenric told him. Then he took off through the hallways, looking for someone, anyone. But they had all gone to the moon ceremony.

He stepped out into the night and tried to puzzle out where the ceremony might be. Dulcet reached up and began running her sharp little claws through his hair. He pulled her hands away. "You don't happen to know where the ceremony is, do you?"

The little hilfen chattered at him, then leaped off his shoulder. She ran ahead a few paces, then stopped to see if he was coming.

As he followed Dulcet, he couldn't get the image of Rindelorn out of his mind. The old Fey's only crime had been agreeing to help Kenric. He'd found something important. Kenric's hand touched the crumpled piece of parchment in his pocket.

Someone hadn't wanted anyone else to know he'd found it. And they were willing to kill to protect the secret.

Kenric's guilt bit painfully into his stomach. He would never have guessed a goal as simple as bringing people together could end up going so wrong.

Dulcet seemed to know where she was going and led Kenric deeper into the forest. Finally, she paused. Up ahead, the sky glowed. The soft light came from the forest itself.

Kenric crept forward cautiously. The Fey had been clear with their warning. He was forbidden to witness this ceremony. But he had to get help for Rindelorn. He scuffed his feet and snapped a twig with his boot, trying to let them know he was there.

No one appeared. He had no choice but to continue forward.

As he approached the large clearing, he got ready to call out, but his breath was struck from his throat.

All the Fey were gathered before him. In the center of the clearing was an enormous tree. Its trunk and branches were silver, its leaves white. The tree glowed, lighting up the forest like midday.

The tree branches were covered with fat white buds. As Kenric watched, they began to open. The buds grew fatter and fatter, then suddenly burst. Brilliant glowing white seeds shot into the air and began to rain down over the Fey. One landed a few feet in front of Kenric.

They weren't seeds. They were moonstones.

With laughing voices, the Fey ran forward to gather the moonstones. Kenric bent over, snatched the one off the ground, and popped it into his pocket. He'd been missing a moonstone ever since his father had left for home. The longer he stayed in Grim Wood, the more sure he was that he'd need the power of all three stones.

Just as he pulled his hand out of his pocket, a voice rang out in the clearing. "Hold!"

All the Fey stopped their gathering and turned toward the voice. Faroth, the captain of the patrol, pointed his finger directly at Kenric.

The Fey turned to look at Kenric. Anger shone in their eyes. He was not welcome here. "I'm sorry to interrupt, but something terrible has happened. Rindelorn has been hurt, shot with an arrow. He needs help."

A large gasp went around the crowd. As one, the Fey turned to King Valorin. He scowled at Kenric, his face drawn into hard, unforgiving lines. "You dare to interrupt our most sacred of ceremonies? Even after you've been warned?"

"Did you hear me? Rindelorn is badly injured. He'll die if he doesn't get help soon."

"To witness this ceremony without the permission of the Fey is treason and your life is forfeit." King Valorin's voice shattered any hopes Kenric had that the king would understand.

"But . . . I needed to find help for Rindelorn!"

The Fey king nodded. "And for that, your death shall be quick and painless. But you have seen something that is forbidden."

Cerinor stepped forward. "I asked him to come, Majesty."

Valorin glared at Cerinor. "You will forgive me if I don't believe you," he said, his voice cold and hard. "I know you will do anything to help this boy in his task."

There was a rustle among the crowd as Linwe stepped forward. "You are right, Father. Cerinor lies. I invited this human tonight."

The crowd of gathered Fey burst into murmurs and gasps at this announcement. The king and Faroth looked at her in horror, as did the rest of the Fey.

Kenric couldn't believe what he'd just heard. Linwe had lied to save him!

"Silence!" Valorin thundered. Then he gave his daughter a look so terrible that Kenric flinched. "You? You have betrayed me? Then you, too, have committed treason."

Shocked silence filled the clearing.

Linwe's face grew pale, but she lifted her chin. "I never meant to betray you. Only to help the human understand the ways of the Fey."

"Bah," King Valorin spat in disgust. He turned to Faroth. "Get them out of my sight."

As the captain of the patrol stepped forward, Dulcet slunk off Kenric's shoulder and scampered over to the nearest tree.

Kenric took two steps, then stopped to call out over his shoulder. "Rindelorn needs help. He will die without it." Then he turned and followed Faroth out of the circle.

❈ 13 ❈

ON THE LONG WALK back to Elga Mora, Kenric had lots of time to think. His heart felt as if it were made of lead. The Fey didn't care that he'd been trying to save one of their people. They cared more about their moon ceremony than Rindelorn's life.

He glanced over at Linwe. She stared down at the ground, a bright spot of color in each of her pale cheeks. He still couldn't believe that she'd put herself at risk in order to save his life.

Or that her father had accused her of treason.

How awful that must feel. Just the thought made him sick inside.

When they reached Elga Mora, Faroth led them down through the root system. After many twists and turns, they stopped in front of a door with wooden bars.

Faroth pulled a key from the ring at his belt and unlocked the door. The guards shoved Kenric and Linwe into the small, dank chamber. "Watch it!" Linwe snapped. "I am still a princess. You may not handle me so."

As the door slammed shut, Kenric ran to it and gripped the bars. "Send someone to check on Rindelorn!"

There was no answer but the sound of the guards retreating.

"And don't harm the goblin!" Kenric shouted out after them. "He was helping!"

As the footsteps faded into silence, Kenric turned around. Linwe stood facing the far wall, her shoulders slumped.

Kenric opened his mouth to say something, then closed it again. How could he comfort her when her father had just called her a traitor? Especially when it was Kenric's fault that she was in this mess. He cleared his throat. "Thank you for standing up for me at the clearing."

Linwe turned, her anger sparking the air around her. "I have never lied to my father before. Never!"

Kenric could only imagine how awful that must feel. "Why did you this time?"

"Because I could not see you killed!"

Kenric gawped. "But you yourself have threatened to kill me many times! This would have been the perfect chance for that."

Linwe turned away from him. She looked down at her hands. "That was before I knew you were telling the truth. Before I knew you really did want to help the Fey." She bowed her head. "And before I knew my father was wrong."

She whirled around and faced Kenric. "I am not sure if I can believe my father anymore! Do you know what that feels like? I can't understand why he is willing to risk Fey lives with his pigheadedness. He is not acting like the father I know."

Kenric could hear the pain in her voice. And there was nothing he could say that would help. It was all true. Her father didn't seem to be thinking of the Fey's safety. His hatred and bitterness had blinded him to the truth. He was so angry that they'd lost a princess nearly a hundred years ago. He couldn't see how he was losing another one to his stubbornness.

"Perhaps your mother will talk some sense into him.

Calm him down," Kenric suggested, trying to think of something to make her feel better.

"I don't have a mother," Linwe said in a small voice. "She died when I was a baby. It is just my father and I."

And now Valorin was acting like he hated her, Kenric thought. He wished again that there was some way he could help.

The sound of footsteps interrupted the silence. The guards had returned. They opened the door just far enough to shove Hnagi into the prison cell. He stumbled, but Kenric caught him. "Are you all right?"

Hnagi gave a miserable nod as the key turned in the lock. "Old skewered Fey still live. They not even say thank you!"

"Well, you did a really good thing today, Hnagi. Thank you."

Linwe sniffed, then looked down at Hnagi. "Did the goblin really tend Rindelorn's wound?"

Kenric glanced at Hnagi, then back at Linwe. "Yes. He stayed with him while I went to find help."

"Is that so?" she asked Hnagi.

It was the first time she'd ever spoken to the goblin directly. Timidly, as if he was afraid of what would come next, Hnagi nodded his head again.

"I would never have thought a goblin capable of such noble kindness." She took a step forward. She screwed her face up, as though she was in pain. "I am sorry I have judged you so harshly," she said in a rush. Then she ignored them and began pacing.

Hnagi stood a little straighter and his face lightened. In spite of their hopeless situation, Kenric's heart swelled. If he could help bridge a gap between Linwe and Hnagi, there might be hope for peace between the Fey and goblins yet.

KENRIC HAD NO IDEA how long they huddled on the cold stone benches. He only knew that time was running out. It was hard not to feel like a failure. He was no closer to any of the answers King Thorgil needed. Nor did he have any idea where Tamaril might be. Worst of all, he had ruined any chance of an alliance with the Fey. Now they would have to face Mordig alone.

There was a noise at the door. Kenric lifted his head as the handle slowly turned.

The door swung open. Cerinor peeked in. The old Fey

lifted his finger to his lips. Then he motioned for the three prisoners to follow him.

Kenric and Linwe exchanged glances. Kenric opened his mouth to speak, but Cerinor shook his head firmly. Kenric woke up Hnagi, then stepped out into the hallway behind Cerinor. Linwe brought up the rear, frowning in puzzlement.

The small group followed the elder Fey through a confusing maze of root tunnels. Once they were far away from their prison, Linwe asked, "How did you get the key?"

Cerinor smiled, and Dulcet poked her head out from under his beard. "Your hilfen has very nimble fingers."

Cerinor finally stopped walking when he came to an old door. He turned and put his hand on Linwe's arm in a comforting gesture. "Your father is being most unreasonable. I don't understand it. I am sorry, feyling. He insists on seeing both your actions as a betrayal."

Kenric felt Linwe shift uncomfortably beside him.

"Half of the elders agree with him, the other half do not."

"What of Rindelorn?" Kenric asked. "Will he live?"

Cerinor nodded his head, a slight smile lifting his features. "Yes, my young human. Thanks to you and your goblin friend, he shall live to study another day. In fact, the council has agreed that he should have a vote in this matter. The king has been forced to hold off punishing you until Rindelorn is strong enough to cast his vote. That should be in a day or two."

"But surely he will agree with our actions?"

Cerinor nodded. "I am certain of it. Which is why I suggested he should have a vote. However, we don't have any time to waste. Too many things point up north to my old friend Thulidor. You must travel to Aryn Dûr and speak with him."

"I forgot!" Kenric said. "Rindelorn was clutching this when I found him." He took the paper out of his pocket and handed it to Cerinor. "A book lay nearby. Some of its pages had been ripped out."

The elder Fey began to read out loud.

"Out of the ancient murky gloom
Three powers arose: earth, fire, and moon.
Each contained within a stone,
Each is needed to keep the throne.
United together brings strength and power,
But twisted in evil brings our final hour."

"Our final hour indeed," said Cerinor. "You say there was a book nearby?"

"Yes, but a whole section had been ripped out. Whoever attacked Rindelorn got the rest of the information we needed."

"I will look into this while you go to Aryn Dûr." Cerinor led them to the door and opened it. Kenric started to step through, but Linwe stopped him. She shook her head, then went first.

She turned back and gave them the all-clear sign. Kenric stepped out into the night with Hnagi right behind him. The moon had set and the dew was falling. It must be near morning.

Cerinor came through the door, then handed Dulcet to Kenric. The old Fey went over to a nearby tree and pulled two packs from behind it. Silently, he handed one to Linwe and the other to Kenric. As they shouldered their packs, he pulled their weapons from his cloak. Linwe's eyes lit up when she saw her dagger. Once they'd strapped on their weapons, the elder Fey stepped forward. He laid his hands on Kenric and Linwe's heads. "Go now," he said. "And may the moon guide your steps and elfspeed bless your journey."

❧ 14 ❧

"So," Kenric asked, "how long will it take to get to Aryn Dûr?"

"The Fey patrol can do it in one day. For us, I'm not sure. It depends." She glanced over at Hnagi. Kenric waited for a snide comment, but there was none. Instead, she turned and headed off into the woods.

"We must hurry. It won't take long for them to figure out where we've gone."

Linwe had no problem finding her way in the dark, and Kenric had no problem following Linwe. She glowed. At first, Kenric thought it was actually her skin giving off light. Then, when she passed under a shadow, she stopped glowing. Kenric realized it was the moonlight reflecting off her skin, not something from inside.

Kenric was glad when the sky began to lighten. The golden light of morning made it harder to think grim thoughts. But his thoughts were dark enough. He feared it didn't matter what Thulidor had to say. King Valorin would still cling to his own beliefs.

When his father had disappeared, it had been dreadful. Kenric's search for him had been full of danger, but the path had always seemed clear. None of it had been Kenric's fault.

This time was different. Things were unbelievably complicated. Some Fey believed him. Others did not. He had brought a deep division to the Fey. He had set father against daughter. He had put friends at risk. Now he had to right a wrong that he'd somehow managed to create.

A harsh caw rang out overhead. "Grymclaws!" Hnagi said as he scrambled for cover.

Kenric flinched and ducked under a nearby tree.

"What of it?" Linwe stopped walking and looked up into the sky.

Kenric stared at her. "Get down!"

"Nasty grymclaw snatch you!" Hnagi warned.

She scowled at them. "What are you talking about? They live on the nearby cliffs, nothing more."

Kenric and Hnagi exchanged glances. "They live here in the forest?"

"Yes. They like the craggy peaks that border Aryn Dûr. But they aren't evil."

"You're wrong," Kenric said. "They're Mordig's servants. One of them captured Hnagi and took him to Mordig. I used one to get into the fortress. Then I had to kill it to escape." He shuddered at the memory. He still had nightmares about it.

Linwe looked puzzled for a moment, then her face cleared. "Didn't you say Mordig had the power to twist men to his cause? It must be the same with the grymclaws. They are just predators, looking for their next meal."

Kenric wondered if that was supposed to make him feel better.

THEY DID NOT REACH Aryn Dûr until after moonrise. Kenric was surprised to find it was nothing like Elga Mora. It was more of a village, if it could even be called that. There was a handful of scattered cottages which were built into the base of large, sturdy tree trunks.

Most of the dwellings looked the same to Kenric. He

had no idea how they would find Thulidor without knocking on a door and asking.

They made a quick pass through the village, then drew away so they could talk.

"I think it's the third door on the left," Linwe said.

"How can you tell?" Kenric asked.

"There's a silver weather vane in front with a complex design. I'm sure it's the work of a master smith. But we still need to be careful. Let's look for a window to peek in so we can be sure it's him."

"You'll recognize him?" Kenric asked. "It's been nearly five years."

Linwe nodded. "True. But I'll remember the shape of him if nothing else."

Puzzled by this, Kenric followed Linwe to the tree house with the silver weather vane. They snuck over to the north side of the cottage. Together, Kenric and Linwe eased themselves up against the window, then peeked inside.

Behind them, there was a whisper of sound. Kenric felt the sharp prick of a knifepoint against his neck. Next to him, Linwe gasped.

"Care to explain why you are spying on me?" a deep

voice asked. Before they had a chance to answer, the voice continued. "Turn around now. Slowly. Let me have a look at you."

Kenric turned around and found himself face-to-face with the most thickset Fey he had ever seen. He immediately recognized the broad chest and shoulders of a smith who had spent a lifetime hammering at a forge.

"Thulidor," Linwe said, her voice flat. She was no doubt mad at being caught unaware.

"How did you know we were here?" Kenric asked.

"You set off one of my alarms. I've been expecting spies for the last five years. Took you long enough to get here."

"We're not spies," Kenric said.

"No? Well, the princess looks like a spy to me. Did your father send you?"

"No!" Linwe said. "He didn't. He doesn't even know I've come."

"I bet that's what you'd say even if he did send you."

"No, really." Kenric stepped in. "Her father has declared her a traitor." He ignored the scowl she gave him and continued. "He even had her thrown in prison. We only escaped because of Cerinor—"

"Ah! My old friend. What's he up to, I wonder."

"Funny, he asked the same thing about you."

"Did he now? Did the old geezer finally figure it out?"

Kenric's spirits rose. It sounded like the old Fey smith did have something he was hiding. Kenric could only hope it would be of some help. "Would the princess be traveling with a goblin if King Valorin had sent her?" he asked. Surely that would convince Thulidor.

"Goblin?" the old Fey repeated in surprise. "Where?"

Kenric looked around, but there was no sign of the goblin. "Hnagi!" he called out.

The goblin shuffled out from behind a tree.

"By the moon!" Thulidor exclaimed. "You'd best come in and tell me your whole story."

The Fey smith gestured them into a small, warm room. A fire burned in the hearth. When Kenric's eyes adjusted to the light, he saw that Thulidor's skin was as rough and wrinkled as old tree bark. His hands were gnarled, and snow-white hair covered his head and chin. As they moved forward into the room, Thulidor stared at Hnagi.

"A goblin, eh? Come out and let me have a look at you."

Hnagi crept out from behind Kenric. He stared at Thulidor with big eyes as the old Fey studied him. Once Thulidor had satisfied his curiosity about the goblin, Dulcet decided she wanted to be friends. She crawled out of Kenric's pack and went over to inspect the smith, then curled up in his lap.

"So, tell me why you're here," Thulidor said at last. "And you might as well make yourselves comfortable while you do it. These sorts of tales are usually long in the telling."

Kenric and Linwe sat down near the fire. They looked at each other. Linwe nodded to Kenric. He took a deep breath and began. "I've been sent by King Thorgil." There was a soft gasp. Kenric looked up from the fire to the old smith. "Did you say something?"

"It was nothing. Continue," Thulidor said.

"King Thorgil has managed to trap Mordig. The warlord is being held in a stone prison, but we don't know for how long. King Thorgil wanted me to talk to the Fey and see if they would ally themselves with us again, as they did long ago. He also needed me to search their ancient lore to see if I could discover information on blades. His sword disappeared when he fought Mordig. Now he needs to find out how to forge another blade of power."

Thulidor shook his head. "He never had a true blade of power."

"How can you be sure? The king said all the kings of Lowthar had thought their sword was a blade of power."

"If it had been a true blade of power, it could have withstood even Mordig's will. The full weight of the three races would be in that blade."

Thulidor leaned forward in his chair and lowered his voice. "Thorgil's sword was forged by human smiths. A blade of power must be forged by all three races."

The old smith leaned back and began to recite.

"The hand of man and the hand of Fey
Linked together will forge the way.
If goblin fires will burn it bright,
The hand of Fey will give it light,
Then blood of man will shape its heart
So land and power will never part."

"This is just what the king was looking for!" Kenric said. Finally he had something of value to report. "Why didn't Marolas know this?"

"Because he is a new smith. My family have been smiths for hundreds of years. We have passed these tales from father to son for as far back as we can remember."

"That information will be of great help to the king. But he also needs the Fey alliance, and King Valorin refuses to help. I have tried to convince him. There is even proof that Mordig's evil is at work here in Grim Wood. But he refuses to see it."

Linwe leaned forward in her chair. "We have seen rot in Mithin Dûr. Some foul poison is killing our trees and ruining our streams. Yet my father does nothing. It makes no sense."

Thulidor looked troubled. "I was afraid of something like this. It was one of the reasons I grew uneasy and left Elga Mora. Two weeks before I left, King Valorin came to me. His bound moonstone was missing—"

Linwe gasped. "It was not! I saw it myself not two days ago."

"She's right," Kenric said. "I saw it, too, hanging around his neck."

The Fey smith shook his head. "No. That is not his bound stone. That is a false stone. A substitute. When he came to me that day, he was so horrified that it was missing, he swore me to silence. He had me forge a new one onto his chain."

"Did he say what happened to his moonstone?"

Thulidor shook his head. "Only that he'd woken up one morning to find it missing."

"My guess is that Mordig found a way to steal it," Kenric said.

"Yes, but we would have known if Mordig had waltzed into Elga Mora and taken the king's moonstone," Thulidor pointed out. "Surely someone would have seen. The king would not have stood there and handed it over. He would have raised a hue and cry. Called for pursuit."

"I don't think you understand just how cunning Mordig can be," Kenric said.

It occurred to Kenric that this could explain King Valorin's odd behavior. "My father told me that if someone else has your bound stone, it makes you vulnerable to them. You feel compelled to do what they say. It weakens your will. Is that true for King Valorin as well?"

Thulidor nodded. "Yes. Which was why he was so beside himself with worry. And why he didn't want the council to get word of this disaster. That's when I knew that something was wrong in Mithin Dûr." He looked down at his own weather-beaten hands. "I would have liked to stay and help put it right, but I had other responsibilities by then."

Linwe shot to her feet. "What other responsibilities do you have, smith? What could be worth abandoning your people?"

Thulidor ignored Linwe's outburst and spoke to Kenric. "It seems I was right, and terrible times have come to Mithin Dûr. Where does my old friend Cerinor stand in all of this?"

"He has been working hard to convince the king to cooperate," Kenric said. "Or at the very least, listen. But his words have fallen on deaf ears. Cerinor has turned all his energies to helping us find the answers we need."

Thulidor studied Kenric's face a long moment. Then he turned to Linwe. "And you say you are on his side? Sworn to bring sense to the Fey, if you can?"

Puzzled, Linwe frowned. "Yes. Why?"

Thulidor sighed, then called out softly, "It's safe. You can come out now."

❧ 15 ❧

THERE WAS A RUSTLE in the shadows. A young woman stepped into the room. She was tall, with long dark hair and strong, proud features. Something about her eyes and nose seemed familiar to Kenric. She gripped her hands together and looked straight at him. "Please, tell me news of my father."

Kenric looked from the young woman to Thulidor. "Princess Tamaril?" he asked.

Thulidor nodded. "She was the responsibility that took me away from Mithin Dûr. Princess, you tell them your story, and then I will tell mine."

Tamaril nodded. "Very well. But please, tell me how my father is," she said, looking at Kenric.

"He is well," Kenric said. "For now. But his struggle with Mordig takes much of his strength."

"Thank you," said Princess Tamaril. She came forward and perched on the edge of a chair. "Now for my story. We had no warning that Mordig was on the march," the princess began. "By the time we found out, his forces were at the gate. We were unprepared and didn't stand a chance."

The princess hugged herself, as if the memory still pained her. "The sound of the battle was terrible," she whispered. "The clang of the weapons, the screams of the wounded. But even when we knew it was hopeless, my father refused to surrender. After two days and nights of fighting, our defenses were utterly destroyed. As Father prepared the soldiers for their last stand, he ordered me to leave.

"I refused. I wanted to stay by my father's side. I wanted to wield a sword and fight this warlord who threatened my home. But Father insisted. He told me his only comfort would be in knowing I was safe. Not wanting to break his heart, I finally agreed.

"He gave me a moonstone, and I grabbed a few supplies. I hurried through the underground tunnels, certain Mordig was nipping at my heels. But I made it to Grim

Wood. My father thought I would be safest there. He was certain that once the Fey knew how bad things were, they would help me." Here her voice faltered slightly.

"It took the Fey patrol two days to find me. They refused to take me before the king as I'd asked. They said my moonstone granted me safe passage. It did not grant me a royal audience. I refused to leave, so they took me to their prison."

"Why didn't I hear of this?" Linwe demanded.

Thulidor raised an eyebrow at her. "This was five years ago, Princess. You were a young child. But this is where I came in. Faroth came to the forge and asked me to make some chains. He wouldn't tell me why, so I went to find out for myself." The smith scowled. "As soon as I saw it was the princess he wanted to imprison, I knew it wasn't right. The stories my family had passed down made it clear. The races were meant to be allies. It was critical that they come together again. Otherwise, they would be weak and vulnerable. But Fey hearts have turned so hard and bitter they have no room for kindness any longer.

"I needed a day or two to make my plans. I told everyone that I had grown tired. I announced that I would go to Aryn Dûr to await my trip across the Silver Sea. Then the princess and I came here. She has lived in hiding while we waited for some sign that it was safe again. Faroth didn't know it was I who freed the princess, but I'm sure he suspected. I have been expecting him on my doorstep for the last five years. But he never came. And now you have."

"But why have there been no reports of it?" Linwe asked as she went over to the window. She peeked out. Satisfied that no one was out there, she turned back to face the room. "Other Fey come here to await their trips across the Silver Sea. Why have they not sent word of the princess?"

"We are not so foolish as to parade her around when others are here. Often, for moons on end, we are the only ones who live in Aryn Dûr. Most stay only a short while, half a moon or so, before making their journey. Our secret was safe enough."

Kenric was quiet as he pondered all that Thulidor had told them. He turned to Tamaril. "That reminds me, Princess. You dropped something while you were in Grim Wood. I have your royal bloodstone. Linwe found it, then gave it to me. Your father wanted me to have it in case I needed the power of all three stones on this journey. But I cannot keep it from you." The idea of the princess feeling beholden to him made Kenric itchy.

"No, my father is right. You must keep it until your tasks are complete. My will is strong, and your heart is pure. I have no fear of you."

Kenric swelled with pride at the princess's words.

Restless, Linwe paced over to the window again. She peeked between the curtains and froze. "They are here."

Kenric whipped his head around. "Who followed us?"

"The Fey patrol," she said, moving away from the window. "Our time is up."

"But surely the patrol will listen to you!" Thulidor protested.

"Not now that my father has declared me traitor," Linwe said. Kenric could hear her struggle to keep the shame out of her voice. "We must make our escape now," she said. "Before we are surrounded."

❈ 16 ❈

Kenric turned to Thulidor. "You must come back with us! Tell the king the things you've told us. If he still doesn't believe, then you must tell the council."

Thulidor frowned. "I am old. I will slow you down. Plus, we must get Tamaril back to her father. She will need an escort through Grim Wood."

"No," the princess said. "I will be fine. I still have a moonstone to guarantee my safe passage."

"But what if it's Faroth who stops you?" Thulidor asked. "Do you think he'll let you get away twice, moonstone or no?"

Tamaril scowled at this complication.

Linwe glanced at Kenric. "With more of us, the journey is bound to take longer."

"But we can't return without proof," Kenric said. "Even if your father chooses to ignore Thulidor, the smith's words will convince the council."

Slowly, Linwe nodded. "True." She grew silent and stared at the wall with a frown. Suddenly, she snapped her fingers and turned to Kenric. "You say you used the grymclaws to carry you into Mordig's fortress?"

"Yes. And they nearly killed me for it!"

She waved that aside. "Grymclaws aren't evil creatures. No more than falcons or hawks or vultures. The ones you met were under Mordig's power."

"You're crazy! I am not going to let a grymclaw carry me all the way back to Elga Mora! They'll kill us before we're halfway there." Kenric turned to Hnagi. "Tell her!"

Hnagi looked thoughtful. "But won't nasty Fey kill us anyway?" he said.

"Yes," Linwe said. "They will kill you on sight."

Hnagi reached out and pinched Kenric. "Use big fat head," the goblin told him. "Ken-ric carry all three stones. Bind grymclaw, just like bind Mordig."

The room grew quiet. All eyes turned to Kenric.

"You have all three stones of power?" Thulidor asked.

Holding on to Dulcet so she wouldn't tumble off his lap, he leaned forward. "May I see them? I have never seen an igni-lith before."

Kenric stared at all the faces looking at him with hope in their eyes. He shrugged. "I guess so." He reached up and lifted the pouch from his neck. He opened it and dumped the stones into his hand. At his touch, the red spots glowed as rich and bright as fresh blood against the dull green of the bloodstone. Beside it, the moonstone glowed faintly. He knew it would light up as bright as the moon if Linwe touched it. Next to it sat Hnagi's firestone. Pale golden lights flickered in its blue depths. Slowly, careful not to touch the moonstone that would burn him, Hnagi reached out and touched his firestone with one knobby finger. The golden lights ignited into brilliant threads of red and gold. The others gasped.

"Do you really know how to use these stones of power?" Tamaril asked. Her voice was soft, as if she was afraid to speak too loudly in the stones' presence.

"Well, I've used them once before," Kenric told her. "Your father showed me how. He must have thought I could use them again. He made me carry them on this journey."

"Very well, then. It is settled." Princess Tamaril's voice rang through the cottage. "We will fly the grymclaws back to Elga Mora."

Thulidor slowly nodded his head. "That will work as well as anything, I guess."

The old smith led them to a trapdoor at the back of his cottage. It opened onto a flight of stairs that went down into darkness. "This will take us to the outskirts of the village," he explained. "With luck, we'll come out on the other side of the patrol."

In silence, they made their way through the short dark tunnel. Kenric was relieved when they finally emerged into the cool night air. He looked over his shoulder and saw the Fey patrol scouring the village and knocking on doors. He jumped when Thulidor tapped him on the shoulder. "Come," the smith whispered. "This way."

They walked in silence until they were well away from the village. When Kenric was sure the patrol wouldn't hear him, he spoke. "How will we get the grymclaws to come to us?"

Linwe gave a sly smile that made Kenric uneasy. "Grymclaws hunt at night. And we have the perfect bait." She nodded her head at Hnagi and Dulcet.

Kenric stared at her a moment. "This is a really bad plan," he said at last.

Hnagi shook his head frantically. His ears flapped back and forth. "Really bad," the goblin agreed.

Linwe shrugged. "It is better than being captured by a furious band of Fey guards. Just think what they might do to our goblin here."

Kenric whipped his head up to look at Linwe. Did she even realize what she'd said? *Our goblin.* She had truly accepted Hnagi!

It wasn't much longer before they reached the foot of the mountain range. They stood in a small clearing while Linwe coaxed both Hnagi and the hilfen to let her tie thick, green vines around their waists. Then she led them to an open space at the base of the cliffs. "You'll be perfectly safe," she explained. "We'll have a hold on these vines the whole time. We won't let them take you."

Kenric could only pray that Linwe knew what she was doing. Hnagi and Dulcet clung to each other, shivering in the dark. "All right. Now what?" he whispered.

"Now we wait for them to take the bait." Linwe grinned.

They didn't have to wait long. Soon, large flickering

shadows blocked out the moonlight. Kenric looked up to find half a dozen black grymclaws circling overhead. One of them called out, the shriek echoing against the mountains. Kenric shivered. Hnagi squealed.

The grymclaws swooped down. Kenric started to jerk the vine back.

Linwe stopped him. "Not yet," she said. "Closer," she murmured. "Closer, closer—*now!*"

Together they yanked on the vine. They jerked the goblin and hilfen out of reach of the grymclaws. Their talons snapped through the air, then they tumbled to an awkward landing. They turned around looking for their escaped prey.

Linwe thrust the vine at Kenric and ran to the grymclaws. They shook their stringy gray hair out of their hideous hag faces and screeched at her. As Linwe spoke to them in her strange, musical tongue, their pale, bulging eyes fixed on her. One of the grymclaws shrieked and stabbed at Linwe with its beak.

Linwe jumped back. "They won't listen to me!" she called to Kenric. "You'll need to use the stones!"

Holding the pouch in his hand, Kenric stepped forward. He kept his eyes on the grymclaws as he reached for the stones. They felt warm in his hand. "Please," he said. "We need you to give us a ride. Back to—"

A loud shriek cut off his words. He jumped back to avoid a slash from a razor-sharp beak.

"Stupid!" Hnagi called out. "Use king's words!"

Hnagi was right. Kenric struggled to remember the exact words the king had used. "By the power of the earth, moon, and fire, I bind you with these stones as they are bound to the king's will, that you may carry us on your backs for as long as we need."

The grymclaw struggled, as if she were waging some inner battle. Then, slowly, one by one, all the grymclaws bent down on one knee.

"It worked!" Linwe called out. "Hurry! Climb on!" As Kenric helped Tamaril onto a grymclaw, Linwe boosted the goblin up onto another one. Once Kenric had settled himself, Dulcet scrambled up to his shoulders. Linwe and Thulidor were the last to mount their grymclaws.

"Okay. We're ready to go," Kenric called out.

With a dizzying lurch, the grymclaw rose up into the air and the ground fell away. Kenric clutched the bird around the neck, afraid of falling off. Air rushed past him, and he felt the motion of the bird's wings against his knees. The grymclaw gave a strangled cry, and Kenric realized he was choking her. He relaxed his grip, but just a little.

Down below, the forest became a blur of treetops. He couldn't believe how small everything seemed. As he looked down, his stomach began to roll. He jerked his gaze upward, not wanting to get sick.

A short while later, Kenric could no longer feel his face. It was numb from the chill night air. His hands felt frozen in place. He was afraid if he tried to move them, they'd crack.

At Linwe's command, the lead grymclaw fell back to fly beside Kenric. Linwe looked as if she were having a great adventure. It made Kenric want to snarl at her.

"It will be time to land soon," she called over to him.

Kenric glanced below, wondering how she could tell. He couldn't see any change in the forest below.

"I thought to have them put us down up by the fouled grove," Linwe called out. "None of the Fey would dare go there at night."

And with good reason, Kenric thought. "No," he called back to Linwe. "It's too dangerous and too far from Elga Mora."

Kenric expected an argument. Instead, she asked his advice. "What do you suggest, then?"

Kenric thought for a moment. They needed someplace the Fey wouldn't think to look for them. A place that was so off-limits they wouldn't even consider it. "How about the lunila tree?"

Linwe looked shocked, then she smiled. "That is perfect."

"Is there a guard posted there that we'll need to worry about?"

Linwe shook her head. "The lunila tree is never guarded." She leaned forward and spoke to her grymclaw, who shrieked out instructions to the others. The grymclaws changed direction and headed west. Kenric's stomach did a nosedive, and he tightened his grip. Never again, he thought. Never again would he hitch a ride with one of these birds.

He spied a faint glow coming from the forest below. The lunila tree's leaves and bark threw off enough light to guide them in.

All too soon the trees grew closer and closer. They rushed by so close Kenric could have reached out and plucked a leaf.

The grymclaws circled once around the lunila clearing, then swooped to the ground. With a jolt that nearly sent Kenric tumbling, his grymclaw landed.

Slowly, creakily, he ordered his muscles to work so he could climb off. Each muscle groaned in agony as he forced it to move. Finally he was standing on firm ground.

He hobbled stiffly over to the grymclaw who seemed to be in charge. He thanked her for the ride. Then he pulled the stones from the pouch around his neck. "With the power of earth, moon, and fire, I release you from my king's will."

The grymclaw shook herself, as if coming out of a trance. The others did the same. Hnagi leaped to his feet and scampered over to hide behind Kenric's legs. The leader let out a piercing shriek. She jabbed at Kenric with her beak. He leaped back, tripping over Hnagi and landing in a heap on the forest floor.

The grymclaw shrieked again, rising into the air as she called out. The other grymclaws followed her.

Linwe motioned them all over to the edge of the lunila clearing. "We can't stay out in the open too long. Who knows what eyes are watching us, even now? Here is my plan. I will go back to Elga Mora, alone—"

Kenric started to protest, but she waved him quiet. "At least hear me out!"

Kenric crossed his arms and nodded impatiently.

"A human or a goblin would be noticed, but I won't. I will make my way to Cerinor and see where things stand. Then we will come back for you and make our case before the council."

Kenric shifted his weight and frowned. He didn't like it.

"She is right," Princess Tamaril told him. "She is able to move faster alone."

"All right," he said. "But we'll need some safeguards. What happens if she doesn't return? What then?"

Linwe glanced up at the night sky. "If I haven't returned by midmorning, you must assume I've been taken. Then all of you should make for the eastern border. Get to King Thorgil as quickly as possible. Tell him what you've learned about the blade. Warn him that the Fey, in their pigheadedness, have refused. But at least your king will have a Fey smith to work with."

"And his daughter," Thulidor added.

Kenric stared at Linwe. "We can't let you take all the punishment for this!"

"You must," she insisted. "If you come to rescue me,

you risk getting captured as well! Then who will report all we've learned to King Thorgil?"

She had a point. But Kenric loathed the idea of letting her go off by herself. "Very well," he agreed reluctantly. He opened his mouth to say something else, in case they shouldn't meet again, but Linwe held her fingers to her lips. Then she turned and slipped away into the forest, making no more sound than the night breeze.

Kenric felt a sharp pinch on his arm. "Ouch!" He slapped down, catching Hnagi's fingers. "Would you quit that?"

"Fey girl being nice," Hnagi said, ignoring Kenric's anger. "Why?"

Still rubbing his arm, Kenric shrugged. "Maybe she's just realized we are trying to help."

"Hnagi not like. Not right, Fey be nice to goblin."

"I thought you'd be happy."

Hnagi shook his head. "Not right. Something tricksie up her sleeve."

Kenric knew deep in his heart that Linwe had risked too much, suffered too much. This wasn't a game to her. "No, you're wrong. She is just finally coming to her senses," he said.

He turned to Thulidor and Tamaril. "Let's find some shelter and rest until morning."

"Sounds good to me," said the old smith. "I could use a nap after that wild ride."

But Kenric found no rest that long night. He was too worried about Linwe. What if Cerinor had been imprisoned for helping them escape? She wouldn't be able to speak with him then. His mind went to the rot spreading ever closer to Elga Mora and the Fey. How long would it take to reach them? And what of old Rindelorn? Kenric could only hope he was still alive.

Kenric stared with wide eyes into the darkness and waited for morning.

BY MIDMORNING, Linwe had still not returned. The Fey must have refused to listen to her. Which meant they wouldn't listen to him, either. He had failed to win their alliance. Humans would have to wage their battle with Mordig alone.

All the excitement Kenric had felt at finding Tamaril and learning how to forge a blade of power seeped out of him. Instead, he was filled with dread at what the Fey might have done to Linwe. He should never have allowed her to face them alone.

She had ordered him to return to Tirga Mor and King Thorgil if she didn't return. He had said that he would, but now he'd changed his mind. She had risked too much to help him. He would stay long enough to help her in return.

He turned to Tamaril, Hnagi, and Thulidor, who sat in the shade of a glinden tree. "She is not coming back."

The old Fey nodded.

"I will not leave her to face this alone," Kenric told him.

"I did not think that you would," the old smith said. Kenric was heartened by Thulidor's trust in him. Tamaril smiled at him, as if his decision did not surprise her, either.

"Here's what we must do," Kenric explained. "Thulidor and I will go to Elga Mora and see what's what. I think you should stay here, Princess. We cannot risk you being captured by the Fey. Your father would never forgive me."

Reluctantly, she nodded her agreement.

"Hnagi keep princess company," the little goblin announced.

"No. I'm going to need you, Hnagi. Thulidor, if it is safe for you to come forward and tell your story, I will signal you. If not, then you must come back here at once. You can escort Princess Tamaril to King Thorgil and help her avoid the patrol. Tell him everything that has happened. Plus, you are a Fey smith. He will need you when the time comes to forge this blade of power."

Slowly, Thulidor nodded. "The chance of a lifetime," he murmured to himself.

"Now come," Kenric said. "Let's see what's happened to that ill-tempered princess."

❊ 17 ❊

KENRIC, HNAGI, THULIDOR, AND DULCET made
their way through the woods. It was a tense, nerve-
racking journey. They flinched at every sound and startled at every gust of breeze. But they were lucky. They
saw no Fey guards on their way.

When they reached Elga Mora, there was still no sign of
the Fey. Cautiously, Kenric moved forward and motioned
the others to follow. He made his way down the main corridor. They approached the throne room and peered
around one of the trees at the entry.

The room was packed with Fey. At the front of the
room, King Valorin stood on the dais. Next to him, Linwe
stood with her head held high. She had silver chains

around her ankles and wrists. Cerinor was there, too, surrounded by guards.

Kenric looked back at the crowd. He would never get through without being seen.

Slowly, he backed away. He turned to Dulcet. "Is there a back door into the king's chambers?" he whispered. "Can you show us?"

Dulcet scampered off down the hallway. She stopped in front of a door built into a hollowed tree. Kenric turned the knob, relieved to find it wasn't locked.

They crept into the king's chambers. Kenric crossed over to the door that led to the throne room. He opened it a crack. King Valorin was listing the charges against Linwe.

Kenric was shocked when he got a close look at the Fey king. He couldn't believe the change that had come over him. He was gaunt now, and a fanatical gleam shone in his eye. For a moment, Kenric thought he saw the king's eyes flash red, but then it disappeared.

Kenric pulled the pouch from around his neck and dumped the stones into his hand. "Earth, sun, and moon," he said to the stones. "Before I can do my king's will, I need to help Linwe. Please help me help her."

The stones grew warm in his hands. The red drops on

the bloodstone became brighter, as if they shone with some inner fire. The moonstone glowed with an intense white light. The firestone shimmered with gold threads that curled up into the air just above Kenric's hand. The warmth spread all through his body.

He folded his hand over the stones then stepped into the throne room.

The Fey who saw him first began to whisper. The whispers grew in volume until the whole room buzzed.

The king whirled around to see what had caused such an uproar. When he saw Kenric, he turned to Linwe. "You said he had returned to his king. You lied to me! Again!"

"She has done nothing wrong," Kenric said, stepping forward. "All she has tried to do is serve her people."

King Valorin glared at Kenric. "Silence! You have brought us nothing but misery." He turned to speak to the crowd of Fey. "He is the one who has poisoned our forest!"

"That is not true, Father! The rot began moons ago," Linwe said.

King Valorin ignored her. "He trespassed on our moon ceremony, when it had been forbidden. He betrayed our trust."

Rindelorn hobbled forward, clutching the arm of a younger Fey. "He did so only to save my life, Your Majesty. I would have died if not for him."

Agitated, the king began to pace. His gaze fell on Hnagi. "He brought a goblin into our midst—"

"Who has done no one any harm," Cerinor said. "And don't forget, Hnagi also helped to save Rindelorn's life. The boy has earned the right to be heard. The council demands it."

The Fey elders nodded their agreement.

Kenric turned to face the crowd. "It is true that evil has found its way into Mithin Dûr," he said. "Your trees rot and your streams are fouled, and this poison spreads. Mordig wants to weaken you, as he has weakened man. Then he will step in to destroy you."

A nervous murmur ran through the crowd. The king strode to the end of the platform. "That is a lie! You told us that you had imprisoned him."

"He will only stay trapped as long as King Thorgil lives. That is why Fey and man need to strike up the old alliance. If you do not believe me, then at least listen to one of your smiths."

Thulidor stepped out of the king's chambers, where he'd been waiting. "What the boy says is true."

A small murmur went up from the crowd.

"I come from a long line of smiths. Our lore has always spoken of the three races working together. Just as three pieces of metal, forged together, make a stronger blade. The same is true of us. If we forge together, we grow in strength."

Rindelorn spoke up again. "The old lore does tell of Fey, man, and goblin working together to fight this evil. I have seen the words with my own eyes."

"See how these three stand together?" Cerinor called out, pointing at Kenric, Linwe, and Hnagi. "Side by side, back to back, and stronger because of it. This is what we all must do."

"Enough!" Valorin shouted as he stepped off the platform. "I am your king. You will listen to me. Ignore these traitors' words."

"How can you say that?" Kenric asked. "We have done nothing to betray you. Linwe is your daughter. She cares for her people." The stones grew hot in his hand. He wondered if they were absorbing his anger.

"When she chose your path, she ceased being my daughter." The king turned to the crowd again. "I am your king. I come from a long line of kings. I have kept you safe, seen to your needs. I have given you no cause to turn against me. Once we slay these traitors, things will be as they were. All will be well again."

As the king spoke, his eyes grew brighter, even more frenzied-looking. His skin seemed to pull tighter over his bones. His eyes flashed red for a moment, and it came to Kenric with a jolt. The king was a Sleäg!

Kenric shook his head. It couldn't be! But how else to explain it?

There was only one way to find out. He gripped the stones so hard that they bruised his hand. He lifted his arm, pointing it directly at Valorin.

There was a sharp hiss as a black arrow whizzed through the air. It missed his fingers by a hairsbreadth.

Kenric whirled around. Faroth, the captain of the patrol, was nocking another arrow to his bow.

⊀ 18 ⊁

THERE WAS A BLUR of motion as a thick body threw itself at Faroth, knocking him to the ground. Thulidor's
massive arms pinned the captain to the floor. The crowd
of Fey gasped and stepped back. The smith looked up at
Kenric and grinned. "Continue."

Kenric faced the king again and lifted his hand holding
the stones. "By the power of the earth, moon, and fire, I
bind you with these stones as they are bound to my king's
will. Free yourself!"

Valorin threw back his head and laughed. "You cannot
stop justice with those ston—"

His words were cut off by a gurgle. His face spasmed,
then he fell to the floor.

Cries of shock rose up from the crowd.

Slowly, wisps of dark gray mist began to rise from his body. They had the same stench as the fouled stream. As they rose, the wisps gathered into a thick, roiling cloud that hovered over Valorin.

The mist moved forward, pulsing and oozing. Dulcet squealed, then leaped off Kenric's back. The room erupted in confusion as Fey began scrambling for the door.

Kenric couldn't let the mist touch anyone. Who knew how powerful its poison was? He needed fire! Fire could evaporate steam. The torches!

Kenric shoved the stones into his pocket as he ran over to the wall of trees. He grabbed one of the moon globes out of its holder. "Hnagi, we need fire!"

Hnagi sprang forward. With one quick strike, the goblin knocked the glowing orb from the torch. It hit the ground with a flash of white light. There was a hiss and sizzle when the released moonlight touched goblin flesh.

Ignoring his burns, Hnagi yanked open the small leather pouch at his belt. He pulled out a handful of his fire-dust and threw it at the wooden stick that had held the moon globe.

It burst into red and orange flames.

Kenric thrust the lit torch high over his head into the oozing black vapor.

The vapor sizzled and hissed in the flame. The smell grew worse. Everyone began to cough. Kenric pulled his tunic up to cover his mouth and nose. He kept his arm high, setting the torch to every bit of vapor he could find.

When at last the cloud was gone, Kenric threw the torch on the ground and stamped out the flames. Cerinor, Rindelorn, and the other elders gathered around the fallen king. Valorin lay deathly still. Linwe was straining at her chains, trying to get to her father. Hnagi stood next to her, patting her hand.

"The keys!" Kenric called to Cerinor as he ran up the steps to Linwe.

The old Fey reached into the king's pocket and tossed the key to Kenric. As they carried the king from the room, Kenric hurried to Linwe's side and began to unlock her chains. She sniffed. "You were supposed to go straight to Tirga Mor."

With a sigh, Kenric looked at her. "Has anyone ever told you that you're bossy?"

Her mouth twitched into an unwilling smile. "Maybe once or twice."

Kenric and Linwe hurried into the king's chambers. Inside, the council had laid the king on a bench. They stood watching him with worried eyes. Linwe scrambled over to her father and knelt beside him.

"I am so sorry," Kenric said. "I never meant to hurt him. I just wanted to get rid of whatever had possessed him."

Linwe wiped at her wet cheeks. "You did what had to be done. He was no longer our king—or my father." She looked over at Cerinor. "What had taken control of him? Do you know?"

Cerinor pursed his lips and stroked his beard. "I do not."

"I think it was Mordig's will," Kenric said. "He has done this to human men. They are called Sleäg. I think the same thing happened to your king. King Thorgil explained it to me. Hatred and bitterness leave people open to Mordig's influence. Once that evil finds a way inside, it makes the hatred burn so hot that nothing of the man, or Fey, remains. That is what I saw in King Valorin tonight."

Kenric's eyes fell on the king's moonstone pendant. He

quickly told the elders what Thulidor had told him about the missing moonstone. "I'm sure that Mordig must have arranged to have the king's bound moonstone stolen somehow."

The council murmured in concern. "Which means he must have spies among us," Rindelorn said, his old face pale. "That is the only way he could have come by the stone. We must mount an investigation at once."

"All the more reason to ally with King Thorgil," Cerinor said. "Our wards and protections are no longer enough."

Kenric dreaded asking his next question. "Do you think Faroth could be behind this? He was the one with the arrows."

Cerinor shook his head. "I don't think so. He is fanatic in his loyalty to the king. I think that blinded him to the wrongness of his actions. But I will look into it."

"What of my father?" Linwe interrupted. "Can we do anything for him?"

"I think he has a chance," Kenric said. "Hopefully, there is enough of his self left that he can recover." A brief vision of his father, broken and bitter in his prison cell, floated through his mind. "But I think that as long as Mordig has his moonstone, he will always be vulnerable."

Just then, the king stirred on the bench. A small moan escaped his lips. Linwe immediately bent closer. "Father? Can you hear me?"

"Yes, Linwe. I can hear you. I'm not deaf. I have a vicious headache, but I'm not deaf."

Linwe huffed out a quick laugh of relief.

"Truly, how are you feeling, sire?" Cerinor asked.

Kenric braced himself for the king's bitter response. But there was none. "I—I'm not sure. My head aches fiercely, and my limbs feel as if they've been turned to water."

"Do you remember what happened, Your Majesty?" Kenric asked.

The king frowned. "Not much. I remember you. And I remember that I was angry at you. And Cerinor." He looked up at the elder. "And Linwe. I remember being furious with Linwe. But how can that be?" He looked at his daughter, clearly puzzled. He took Linwe's hand and patted it.

A look of relief passed around the council.

"Do you remember losing your moonstone?" Kenric asked gently.

The king clutched his pendant. His eyes widened in surprise. "How did you know?"

"Thulidor told us." Linwe spoke softly. "He explained how you had him fashion a new one."

The king's face flushed. "I was so shocked that I had lost it! It has been handed down to Fey kings since our beginning! I—I was ashamed."

"We don't think you lost it," Kenric said. "We think Mordig found a way to steal it," he explained.

By the time the king had heard the whole story, he was exhausted.

"He must rest now," Rindelorn said. "Sleep and a little moonwort should do wonders."

"True," Linwe agreed. She gave her father a kiss on the cheek, then stood. She held her head high and straightened her shoulders. "I must address the Fey. They need to know what has happened."

She turned and walked back out into the throne room. Kenric followed. When the Fey saw her, a hush fell over them. "As you have all seen, my father has taken ill. It was an illness born of Mordig's evil. Those who have claimed that this Mordig is not a Fey problem have been proven wrong." Linwe turned to Kenric. He was struck by how well the mantle of ruler settled across her shoulders. "Kenric of Penrith, you may tell your human king that the Fey pledge their full support against this evil. In truth, we have waited too long."

Kenric's heart swelled. He *hadn't* failed!

Suddenly Linwe smiled, and she looked more like the Fey girl he'd known and argued with. "Besides, if all the humans have half as much heart as you, we shall be lucky to call them friends."

THEIR SMALL PARTY ARRIVED at Tirga Mor just before sunset two days later. They had been so anxious to get home, they had traveled almost without stopping. Kenric was nearly bursting with all the news he had for the king. And he couldn't wait to see his face when he presented Tamaril.

The guards at the gate ushered them straight through. Linwe and Thulidor slowed down, staring at the castle around them. Kenric forgot they had never seen a castle before. "Hurry up," he said. "I'll give you a tour later."

Kenric led them to the king's chambers. He gave a quick rap on the door. "Come in," the king's voice called out.

Kenric took a deep breath, then threw open the door. "We are back, Your Majesty." He nearly gasped when he saw the king. Thorgil looked older and more frail than he had a few days before. Worry began to gnaw at Kenric's gut. "W-we have good news."

The old king's face brightened. "Come in and share it with me, then. And introduce me to your companions," he said as he spied Thulidor and Linwe.

"The Fey have agreed to ally themselves with us. I learned much from them about the forging of a blade of power. And they've sent their master smith, Thulidor, to help us. The Fey princess, Linwe, has also agreed to help." Linwe gave a small, formal bow before the king.

At the word *princess,* the king's face fell slightly. Kenric hurried on. "And, perhaps best of all, I have someone who is very anxious to see you."

At his cue, Tamaril stepped into the room. The king rose quickly, knocking his chair over. His face shone so brightly that Kenric had to look away.

Tamaril ran into her father's arms, and he caught her in a giant hug. Kenric felt a lump growing in his throat. He saw a movement out of the corner of his eye. Linwe was wiping away a tear. She caught him looking, and scowled.

Kenric felt a grin spread across his face. He couldn't help it. They had come through so much together.

But he knew it was not over. Not yet. He stopped smiling and sighed.

If the Fey lore was correct, they needed the goblins' co-operation as well. And Kenric couldn't help but think there must be some evil at play in the goblin realm. Mordig had made bold moves against the Fey and human kings. There was no reason to think he'd spared the goblin king. Whoever that was.

Kenric had a feeling he would soon find out.

THE ADVENTURE CONTINUES IN BOOK 3

THE TRUE BLADE OF POWER

LATER THAT NIGHT, just as Kenric was getting ready to crawl into bed, there was a knock at his door. He quickly pulled his tunic back on and went to open it.

It was one of the palace guards. "The king requests that you come to his chamber at once."

"Of course," Kenric said. As he followed the guard, he wondered what new surprise awaited him.

When they reached the king's chambers, the guard opened the door. Kenric stepped into the dark room. The three torches against the wall flickered in the draft. "You sent for me, Your Majesty?"

King Thorgil nodded. "I did. Hnagi and I have been talking." The king waved the little goblin forward. Kenric stepped back in surprise. He hadn't seen him there, standing in the shadows.

The king leaned back in his chair. "You accomplished much in Grim Wood, but we are not finished yet."

Kenric nodded.

"There has been no contact with the Goblin King since my father's time. I've been questioning Hnagi about the goblins and their affairs. He has given me some information, but it is not enough. He has, however, agreed to be your guide to Carreg Dhu, the goblin realm. Once again, I must call on you to be my ambassador. Even with Fey and Man allied, it will not be enough to defeat Mordig. If we are to have a chance at success, the goblins must join us as well."

Kenric swallowed nervously. The idea of this journey made him uneasy.

"I am even more worried now that I know Mordig has two royal stones of power, mine and King Valorin's," the king continued. "His powers grow even as ours weaken. We do not have long. I had hoped for a few years to set things right. Now I see it will be months—possibly only weeks or even days. There is no time to lose."

"Do you want me to ask their permission to forge the blade of power on the goblins' fires, Your Majesty?"

"Yes, that first. Then you must try to convince them to join forces with us. I will not mislead you. This will be harder than it was with the Fey. The Fey only needed to be convinced to ally with Man. The goblins must be convinced to ally with Man and Fey. The Fey have been their enemies now for over a hundred years."

Kenric glanced uneasily at Hnagi. He didn't want to offend the little goblin, but he had to know. "Is there a chance the goblins are working with Mordig?" he asked the king.

"That had occurred to me as well, since they share a border." The king turned to Hnagi. "What do you think?"

Hnagi scowled. "Mordig make raids on góblins. Steal for slaves. Góblins not like Mordig," he said, shaking his head firmly.

King Thorgil frowned. "But we cannot be certain." The king closed his eyes for a moment, as if the effort of talking had exhausted him. When he opened them again, he looked directly at Kenric. "I know you are anxious to get home, but once again, your kingdom needs you."

"Very well, Your Majesty." Kenric looked at Hnagi. "Into the goblin realm we shall go."